Dream Journal

KAREN HALVORSEN SCHRECK

HYPERION BOOKS

NEW YORK

First Edition

1 3 5 7 9 10 8 6 4 2

Printed in the United States of America

Library of Congress Cataloging-in-Publication Data on file.

ISBN 1-4231-0105-7 (hardcover)

Reinforced binding

Visit www.hyperionbooksforchildren.com

For Josephine and Clayton Halvorsen

And for Greg

JUNE 30

It's raining umbrellas. The little paper ones that usually come with tropical drinks, and always decorate the hot fudge sundaes at her favorite diner. Black strokes mark their colorful tissue—Chinese characters, she once said, the symbols for luck and long life. The umbrellas open and close like butterfly wings, rustling, tearing; toothpick ribs creaking, snapping. The shower becomes a storm I can't escape.

"Will she die?" I asked over dinner.

Dad covered his face for a moment, then lowered his hands and looked at me, his eyes tired and red.

"Yes," he said.

I think he meant soon, though he didn't say this. For three weeks now, a hospital bed has pushed back the other furniture in our living room. We keep the bed's wheels locked so it won't roll away. Mom lies there all the time, growing smaller. Sometimes she is so still, I can't see her breathing beneath the covers. Other times she thrashes around, trying to get comfortable, I guess. She kicks off the covers, and finally falls asleep with her limbs all twisted like something hit by a car—something made of skin and bones and nothing else.

I'm so tired—tired for no reason—like last night and the night before. Crashed on my bed again. Only tonight is different. For the first time, I've opened this journal. I've written down my question and Dad's answer. His "yes." I've made it real. The long shadows nod, *Yes. Yes*, the wind hisses through the willow's branches. *Yes*.

No.

In eight weeks, it's my birthday. I'll be seventeen, nearly a junior, because the following day school starts. According to last year's idiotic personality assessment test (the result being that I would make a great nun), I like to set goals and I like to be prepared. Maybe that's why I vowed to ask Dad about Mom before too much more time passed—before I woke up and realized that I was no longer sixteen, and Mom was no longer alive. My goal was to Be Prepared. Maybe I should be a Boy Scout instead of a nun.

But it's hard to be prepared when you've got the

shakes. When I even thought of asking Dad about Mom, I trembled like I'd been left out in the cold. I felt like I was leaning over a deep, dark hole. I tried to imagine something inside the hole, something to fill it. All I came up with was empty.

So tonight I put down my forkful of dinner and asked before I could even think. And now I believe that the hole closed up with Mom inside, far away, finally gone. I bet I won't even dream about her, the way I used to every night.

JULY 1

I can't fold the sheets. The ends won't match up. White cotton bunches, wrinkles, and sags. I try to smooth the seams, but I only make things worse. The ends won't match up. White cotton bunches, wrinkles, and sags. I try to smooth the seams, but I only make things—

"Tell her I'm sleeping if she asks," Dad said. "I'm sleeping right upstairs." He stood at the back door, his hand on the latch. "Tell her I don't feel well. I'm taking a little rest."

Dad gives Mom everything, until he's got nothing left to give. Then he runs away. This happens once a week or so. Usually he goes to some school function, where he can be his Coach Self, not his Husband or Dad Self. I know because I've heard about his escapades through kids at school—kids I hardly know, who know Dad better than I do. "Your dad's so cool," a second-string lineman once said—make that *gushed*—"the way he helped us paint the locker room. We thought we'd never get done, and then he shows up and puts some real muscle into it." Or, according to a first-string fullback: "Your dad's not afraid of anything. He was chaperoning the team's booth at the county fair, you know"—I wouldn't know, but I'm good at pretending—"and afterward, he went on that intense roller coaster over and over again. You should have been there."

Well, I wasn't there. These days I hardly ever go out, even when Dad is home and I'm not needed. I'll walk to the library; sometimes I'll see a matinee. But only if I'm up for running into one of Dad's groupies. Mostly it's better to stay in my room like I am right now, on my bed with this journal—though usually I'm here with a book that's big enough to pass for a wall. I've read *Gone with the Wind* three times in the last two months. I found a musty copy in the basement. From the peeling bookplate, I know that *This Book Belongs to Grace Mills*. Mills was Mom's maiden name. The handwriting must be hers, too, though I don't recognize it. It's hard for me to believe that Mom wrote like such a girl, all loop-de-loops and curlicues. It's hard for me to believe that Mom *was* a girl. But her fingerprints, reduced a size or two, smudge the margins, and pages are dog-eared at the bottom corner. "Nasty habit," she used to tell me, as she marked her place that way. "Don't let me ever see you doing this. Never ever."

I haven't talked to anyone about what's happening to Mom. Don't want to. Can't. Dad doesn't talk about her either. He said one thing to me when she first got sick: "Whatever happens to your mother, it's private. It stays inside this family. We don't go airing our dirty laundry— our troubles, I mean." As for Mom, well, from the start I could tell she didn't want anyone to know. For a long time, she didn't do anything but sit in the living room with the shades drawn, a wig perched on her head like a big, molting bird. She kept her arms crossed over her chest like she was ashamed of what was happening there. Whenever he could, Dad kept watch beside her.

It was early afternoon when Dad left today, and Mom was asleep. I've been alone with her before, but usually Dad gives me a little warning. Not today. He raked his hands through his thick brown hair and rattled off all the things I already know: if Mom wakes up, give her the bedpan; offer her Jell-O or tapioca pudding; if that doesn't work, soak one of those little sucker sticks, with a tiny pink sponge on the end, in ice water and let her suck on that; if she gets restless, turn on the TV.

"Remember," Dad said, "she likes sports. There's a

gymnastics competition on channel two. She'll like that."
And then, *bam*, he bolted, jogging across the driveway to
the car.

I wanted to remind Dad that Mom won't talk to
anyone but him these days. He finishes sentences for her.
He's the one who knows what she's really trying to say.

"Your hair is sticking up," I called instead. Anything
to stall. "Maybe you should comb it?"

Dad stood by the car, keys in hand. "Has she ever
once woken up?"

I shook my head.

"So." Dad opened the car door. "She won't even know
I'm gone. But *if* something happens and she does figure
it out, tell her I'm sleeping right upstairs and I'll be
awake by dinner."

I watched Dad pull out of the driveway. Then I went
back into the house and of course something happened.
Mom's bell rang. It's a little brass cowbell, engraved with
edelweiss—a souvenir from when Mom and Dad were
newly married and living in Austria on an army base. The
only photograph that Dad carries in his wallet is a well-
worn snapshot that shows Mom standing at the top of a
mountain. She's wearing lederhosen (!) and holding the
bell up like a trophy. Her smile makes me uncomfortable.
It's devilish and knowing. Okay, it's sexy. She looks

7

like she'd never need to use that bell for anything but fun.

Until today, I have only answered the bell when Dad is home, but occupied—talking on the phone maybe, or mowing the lawn. Then all I do is tell Mom, brightly, "He'll be right here!" And he is right there. He takes over, and I stand back. I stand back behind him, waiting for him to tell me what to do, how I can help, what Mom needs. But all Mom ever needs is Dad. He bends over her, smoothing a sheet, fluffing a pillow, doing small things with his hands that I can't see. I stand back and back and back, until I find I'm standing in the hallway. Then I go lie down on my bed and read *Gone with the Wind*.

After a few minutes of silence, during which I actually prayed that Mom had gone back to sleep, the bell rang harder, *tonk, tonk, tonk*—a clanking cowbell sound that I'd never heard before, because Mom's first ring never goes unanswered. I walked slowly toward the living room. I was pissed off all of a sudden, and when I get pissed off, I have a tendency to drag my feet. But finally, there she was, lying on her back in the hospital bed, clutching the bell's red leather handle in both hands. She swung the bell up, down, up. *Tonk, tonk, tonk.*

"Mom," I said.

She turned wildly and the bell went flying. It rolled

8

under the coffee table and whacked against the wall. Mom stared like she had never seen me before.

"Pan," she said.

"What?" My voice came out icy.

Mom grabbed the sheets. "Bed." She twisted the sheets. "Pan."

"What?"

"Now!" she said.

I understood then. I knelt and pulled the bedpan from beneath the bed. It was cold and heavy and awkward to hold.

"Now!" Mom said. She shoved her thin hands from the sheets, clutched my wrists, pulled. The bedpan wobbled and I almost dropped it.

"Help me," she cried.

Blood pounded in my head; the sheets blurred and rippled like water. Think, I thought. Think. I balanced the bedpan on the edge of the mattress, put one hand under Mom's hip, put my other hand under her other hip, and slowly lifted her. When she was high enough, I nudged the bedpan into place. She winced at the touch of metal—there are bedsores on her tailbone, raw and open—then she turned her face away.

"Okay," she finally said.

I lifted her again. I pulled the bedpan out. Dry.

Mom wouldn't look at me. She looked at the ceiling instead—at a brown water stain that I'd never noticed before. I took a deep breath and set the bedpan on the floor.

"Would you like some Jell-O?" I asked.

"Warden," she said.

My father's name. She whispered, so I could barely hear it.

"He's sleeping. He's not feeling well, so he's taking a little rest. But don't worry, he'll be awake soon." I swallowed hard. "How about some tapioca pudding?"

She didn't move.

"Okay." I pushed my sweaty bangs from my forehead. "Dad said you'd like this."

I walked to the TV and turned it on to channel two. Brassy music swelled as colored rings rippled across the screen. The Olympics. I'd forgotten they were on.

Mom let out a low moan and a sour smell filled the room. I stared at the TV. A girl in a green leotard backflipped across a blue mat, then did a tight somersault in the air. She landed in the splits at the mat's edge, her arms in a perfect V. She stayed like that for a moment, every muscle taut and defined. When the audience applauded, the girl leaped to her feet and bowed.

Mom moaned again. From the corner of my eye, I

watched her head toss on the pillow. Her hair separated into greasy, lank pieces. *No,* I thought she was saying. But what I heard her say instead was, "Please?"

"Okay," I said. I went to her. She had wet the bed. "Okay," I said again. I waited like she would tell me what to do.

"I'm sorry," was all she said.

Her eyes were wider and darker than I've ever seen them. They reminded me of the eyes of a deer that Dad and I hit on the way home from school last fall, the one day we left Dad's old Bonneville in the garage and drove Mom's red Firebird convertible instead. Dad bought the Firebird for Mom right after she got sick. He must have thought a flashy vintage car would make her feel better, make her forget, make her happy again. He never drove the Firebird until this particular day, when he explained to Mom that he had "to keep the engine alive." He smiled nervously as he said this, like he was betraying Mom somehow. But she just nodded okay, whatever.

She hadn't driven the car for months, but it still smelled like roses. Like her. On the way home that night, I started to open my window and Dad said sharply, "Don't." I got a little huffy, but then I realized he was right: this was better than fresh air. The headlights were changing the brown leaves to gold, and we were sailing

11

along just like old times. Except Dad was there instead of Mom.

Then a deer flashed across the right side of the car's hood. A doe, just her head, that's all I saw. Her head was elegant, like something carved out of glossy wood, with an ebony nose. I saw the delicate black lines of her mouth, the soft pink insides of her flared ears, her eyes. Then there was a thud, the Firebird lurched, and leaves swirled again before us. The doe had vanished.

Dad pulled the car over and got out. He told me to stay inside, but I couldn't. I ran around to the front of the car where he stood. The right headlight was shattered, the side mirror hung by wires—red and blue wires like arteries and veins. A smear of blood gleamed deeper red, almost black across the red door, and from the handle hung a hunk of brown fur.

We walked maybe half a mile back down the road, but the doe was nowhere to be seen. Dad stared into the cornfields that surrounded us. The bare stalks rattled in the wind. "Gone," he said. "Long gone. Nothing we can do to help her now."

The wind was cold on my throat. "Will she be all right?"

"Maybe. Or maybe she'll go quickly and mercifully. I hope." Dad put his hand to his chin, rubbed the rough growth of stubble there. I shivered and felt, more than saw, Dad's glance.

"Come to think of it," he said, "the impact couldn't have been that bad. Our car would be in a lot worse shape if she'd been hit harder. Maybe she will be all right."

He patted my shoulder, which made me flinch. He hasn't touched me much this last year. Quickly, he took his hand away. "Don't upset Mom with this," he said gruffly. "I'll get the car fixed so it'll look like it never happened."

I didn't tell Mom and he did get the car fixed, and now the Firebird looks like nothing ever happened. Except something did—something I saw in Mom's eyes today. Her eyes were an animal's eyes, wide and deep enough to drop into, trusting and fearful at the same time. When Mom looked at me with those eyes, I put my hand on her forehead and touched the sharp bones above her temples. I stroked down over her eyelids, brushing them closed.

"Hush," I said. "It'll be all right."

She kept her eyes closed while I changed the sheets. I saw Dad do this once before. He didn't know I was watching. I stood in the hallway and studied his practiced movements, the tender, quiet way he smiled and joked with Mom to keep her from feeling ashamed.

Now I tried to do the same. I rolled Mom gently from one side of the bed to the other, pulling the sheets from the bed when her body was out of the way. "Upsy-daisy," I kept repeating—something Mom used to say to me when I was a little girl. I settled her back onto the sheepskin pad Dad keeps on the mattress for her bedsores. Then I ran to the basement, tossed the soiled pile in the washer, ran upstairs to the linen closet, grabbed a clean set of sheets, ran back to the living room, and rolled her gently this way and that again, putting the clean sheets on the bed. She didn't open her eyes once; at least not while I was in the room. But she was awake, I could tell, from the sighs she let escape while I worked.

"There," I said, when everything was in place. I was really sweating now.

Mom opened her eyes and said, "Turn off the TV, Livy."

I had forgotten the TV was on. Now some other wiry girl was sprinting toward a vault; she sprang up, landed on the vault on her hands, spiraled from it through the air, and hit the mat square on her feet, to thunderous applause.

"I hate gymnastics," Mom said.

I opened my mouth in surprise, but couldn't think of what to say.

"Watch out," Mom said. "A fly might fly down your throat."

I laughed. Mom always used to make that crack about the fly.

"A fly *might* fly down your throat." Mom smiled wistfully, like the fly was something she'd lost and longed for. We looked back at the TV. A Coke commercial was on now. People singing together in peace and harmony.

"Turn it off, Livy," Mom said.

"But Dad told me—" I began.

"Your dad's wrong." Mom tossed her head again, but only for a moment. Then she looked at me with eyes more like her own, eyes that understood this moment completely—still wide and dark, but not an animal's. "All those kids whirling around, all those perfect tens. Why would I want to stare at that? Your Dad likes to stare at that. Not me."

"Never? You never liked it?"

"I tolerated it because he loves it—no, he *lives* on it. I never liked it. Oh, Livy, enough. Pull the plug on that thing. I can think now. We can talk a bit."

I went and turned off the TV. As soon as the screen blinked to black, Mom groaned. I ran to her.

"What's wrong?"

"Nothing." She tightened her lips, biting back

another groan, but I heard it, deep inside her throat. "The morphine's worn off, that's all. Your dad never lets it wear off. I guess this is why."

"I'll call Mrs. Ford."

Mrs. Ford lives across the street. She's a registered nurse, who works nights so she can be with her four kids. She's got her hands full, what with them and her loud, cheery husband. But in the last week, she's come over to our house every few hours, or whenever Dad calls her (whichever comes first), to give Mom a shot of morphine. Mrs. Ford gives Mom other medicine, too, syrups and pills I don't know much about, except that they seem to ease Mom's hacking cough. And if Mom's cough is too bad by the time Mrs. Ford arrives, she hooks Mom up to the oxygen mask that dangles from the metal tank by the hospital bed.

"I'll call Mrs. Ford right now." I turned to go. In my mind, I could see the piece of pink paper posted above the kitchen phone that had three things written on it in Dad's cramped handwriting: numbers for the doctor, the ambulance service, and Mrs. Ford.

Mom caught my wrist. "No, Livy."

I turned back slowly.

"I can't talk through morphine. Sit down here beside me."

16

"But—"

Mom managed a smile. She drew me closer to the bed. I leaned against the mattress, careful not to bump her. It was almost like sitting.

"Remember how we used to talk?" Mom said.

At that moment, I couldn't exactly remember. But I nodded.

"I remember." Mom furrowed her eyebrows; a little tree of lines branched between them. "I remember we used to talk a lot."

"We'd talk about school," I offered. We must have talked about school sometimes.

"Yes!" The lines between Mom's eyebrows vanished. "Let's talk about school! What are you studying now? What's your favorite subject?"

"It's summer, Mom. I'm on vacation." And besides, I wanted to say, those are the kind of questions a distant relative asks me, someone I see maybe once a year at Thanksgiving.

But I'm glad I didn't say that, because what I did say made Mom feel bad enough. Suddenly, her eyes held tears.

"I forgot," she said. "I forgot it's summer. It's hot, isn't it? I don't think I even knew."

"It's okay, Mom. It's no big deal."

Her hands lay quietly on the sheets. I covered

them with mine. My hands are bigger than hers, now.

"It's no big deal," I said again, my throat tightening. "Okay, let's talk about school last spring. I liked my English class pretty well. My teacher got us thinking about doing journals. Remember that journal you gave me? Well, I'm using it."

"Really?" Mom's face was open and eager.

Ever since Dad told me you were going to die, I thought.

Write down your dreams, Mom had said when she gave me this journal. A year ago. Just before cancer. Have lots of wonderful dreams, write them in your journal, and let the dreams tell you what they mean.

Now Mom said, "It's blue. Isn't it?"

It's red, her favorite color, but I didn't say this. I nodded and Mom sighed, relieved.

"My teacher made us read Greek myths." Even my voice sounded tight. I took my hands from Mom's and rubbed my throat for a minute. Better. "All the girls had to do reports on Persephone—she's the one who got carried off by the king of the underworld." I hadn't put more than two or three words together with Mom in months, and now the words tumbled out of me like this was a game show and I was a contestant and the clock was ticking. "She—Persephone—had to marry this king and stay

18

in his kingdom of Hades, and her mom, Demeter, got so upset that she cursed the harvest until famine plagued the land. Demeter searched and searched for her daughter. Years passed and Demeter kept right on grieving. She wouldn't take off her mourning clothes."

Mom flung her arm over her eyes like the light had gotten too bright.

"Don't worry," I said quickly. "Persephone ultimately gets rescued. I can't remember how, exactly. But that's not what's important. What's important is that Persephone gets to spend half the year aboveground with her mom. What's important is the happy ending."

"Your English teacher." Mom lifted her arm from her eyes and lowered it slowly to the bed. "That would be Mr. Stockton, right? He would have been your teacher last spring. Dad always got along well with him. Oh, except Mr. Stockton's not very good about letting team members leave class early for away games, right?"

Mr. Stockton was my teacher in eighth grade, two years ago. He doesn't teach high school.

"That's right, Mom," I said quietly. "Mr. Stockton."

Mom nodded and smiled. "Tell me more about last spring."

What could I say? Could I tell her: I hardly remember last spring, if you want to know the truth. I remember the solarium at the hospital and doing every puzzle there, piece by piece, then doing some of them again; waiting while Dad visited you, because the doctors didn't like me in the room, afraid I would stir you up too much, they said. Could I say: let me tell you about the butterfly puzzle, the cheeseburger puzzle, the puzzles of postcard places we've never been?

"Have you ever read *Gone with the Wind*?" I asked.

Mom pushed herself up on her elbows, groaning as she did so, but smiling, too. "I loved that book when I was your age. What did you think?"

And that was it. That was the way we used to talk. I remembered now. We used to talk like talking was easy. I leaned closer to Mom. I could hardly wait to tell her what I thought. "Well," I began.

The doorbell rang. We stared at each other. We didn't move. The doorbell rang again. Mom turned her face toward the wall. I couldn't remember anymore what I thought about *Gone with the Wind*.

"I have to find your bell before Dad comes home." I caught my breath. "Before Dad wakes up, I mean."

"My what?"

"Your cowbell. You dropped it. It rolled under the couch, remember?"

"Oh." Mom sighed wearily. "Oh," she said again,

only this time, it wasn't a word. It was a sound from someplace dark and hidden, where the pain was.

The doorbell rang a third time.

"I'd better get that," I said. "It might be Mrs. Ford."

Mom's head tossed on the pillow. White flecks of spit dotted the corners of her mouth. I ran to the door, opened it.

But it wasn't Mrs. Ford standing there in the harsh sun, summer leaves green in the background, summer grass singed brown. It was my best friend, Ruth Walker, her hair flaring out like a burst of white light.

JULY 2

A Herd of kids, huddled together for comfort or
warmth. *Don't look at me, I'm not here.* I want to
hide. But I can't.

Sure enough, in a single, slow movement, they
turn.

Things aren't any less scary because they're pre-
dictable.

The kids don't have faces.

*Y*ou've got to have a best friend to even survive at my
school, unless you move in a Herd. If you move in a Herd,
you've got nothing to worry about. The Herd will be
your best friend. It'll be family, bodyguard, and God too.

Ruth and I are survivors, I guess. Or you could
say that we've been each other's Herd. A Herd of two.
She's a PK—a pastor's kid. My family's pastor's kid, actually. Dad used to say (ominously and with only a tinge of

irony), "Your mother and I sewed our wild oats in our twenties, and then *the fear of the Lord descended upon us.*" Turns out, they got religion when I was born, and they promptly joined the Troy City Bible Church, shepherded by the then wavy-haired, now bald-as-a-cue-ball Pastor Bob Walker. Ruth and I were baptized on the same day— "Dunked," Ruth calls it. We came up for air screaming, and each of us in turn took a bite out of Pastor Bob's boutonniere. Pastor Bob always used to say (not at all ominously and with a lot of irony) that this event was our first communion. Ruth and I just think of it as the beginning of a beautiful best friendship.

Seeing each other on Sundays has helped Ruth and me understand that we are bigger than school. Bigger than the girls with better hair and better clothes. Bigger than the boys that never liked us back. Bigger than the names that Herds called us on the playground, and, more recently, in the hallways.

"Bible Banger," "Holy Roller," "Saint Ruth." From the start, Ruth got called a lot of names that had nothing to do with her, and everything to do with her father. Nobody was ever stupid enough to slam my father, so my names have had everything to do with me. I happen to be skinny and extra tall (still one inch shy of six feet, thank God), with straight, flat, do-nothing, dark hair, and arms and legs that go everywhere but where I want them to go. Naturally, I get called "Olive Oyl" instead of Olivia, along with "Bolivia," "O Trivia," "Chlamydia," and "Gigantica," which doesn't rhyme great, but packs a punch, let me tell you.

In spite of what everyone says about her, Ruth is not a Goody Two-Shoes priss. She believes in God, but she believes in God in her own doubtful way. At church, she sits in the back pew with her arms folded. She may not look like she's listening, but she is, and she's watching. Later, she asks some seriously serious questions.

Ruth stopped asking me serious questions around the time Mom got sick, when she realized I wouldn't answer them. I knew if I so much as opened my mouth, I would *air our dirty laundry—our troubles, I mean*. Ruth and I didn't talk about the change—the shift from knowing everything about each other to knowing next to nothing. Sometimes she babbles on about things she knows neither one of us really cares about—hairstyles and lip gloss and diets. I listen to her babbling, but after a while, I guess my eyes glaze over or something, because she always gets flustered and makes some excuse to say good-bye. It's better when we just go to a movie, where we don't have to say much at all.

I didn't say anything when I opened the door yesterday and saw Ruth. Instead I immediately closed the door to a crack.

"Well, hi to you too." Ruth wedged her foot in the doorway. She took a deep breath. "I'm *centering* myself," she used to say, when she breathed like this, and then she'd roll her eyes, like, *just kidding*. But now she forced a fake smile. She didn't look terribly centered, with her foot jammed in the door.

"I've been missing you, Livy. Where have you been?"

"I've been kind of busy." From down the hall came the sound of Mom moaning.

"I guess so." Ruth stopped smiling. She nervously tucked her bushy hair behind her ears. In the summer, the sun bleaches Ruth's blond hair and the humidity whips it up wild. Ruth is always trying to straighten her hair with a curling iron. Yesterday, like most days, she failed. Her hair was flat on top and kinky on the sides, with sharp edges ironed into the back. There was a red burn mark on her neck that looked exactly like a hickey. Ruth saw me staring at the mark, and she stared right back at me until I had to look away. Ruth's hair may be lame, but her gaze is a powerful thing. Her eyes are beautiful—almond-shaped, with irises so intensely blue they're almost purple, and long lashes that curl up at the end. I used to tell her all the time that her eyes were

25

the windows to her soul, but she always shrugged it off, like, Who cares, if you're the only one who thinks so?

"So what are you doing for the Fourth of July?" Ruth shifted her weight, but she didn't move her foot. "Since you're so busy, you must have plans."

"I plan on being unpatriotic."

"Oh, come on. The Fourth only happens once a year. And we always go to the parade. *Together.*"

I put my hand over my heart. "I'll recite the Pledge of Allegiance forward and backward."

"Yeah, right." Ruth glanced at the driveway. Kids were sitting there in a car I didn't recognize, a rusted, green sedan. Ruth waved, and someone lifted a shadowy hand and waved back. "I'll be right there," Ruth shouted, then looked at me. "At least come help finish the float tomorrow night. There's going to be a great party at Chloe's, in her barn."

Chloe Cunningham is the richest, prettiest girl in our class. She is also class president, and thus, a major force in the Student Government Herd. Every significant class event happens at her house, in the basement or swimming pool or barn.

"Let's see," I said. "What would be more fun? Tearing my fingertips open on chicken wire or having an allergic reaction to all that hay?"

Ruth laughed like old times. "Now, now. Don't knock the float until you've seen it. You probably don't realize that the subject matter is deadly serious—all military, all the time—in honor of our country's fighting forefathers and our own fighting Trojans. We're making a battering ram. It looks very real, like it could do some damage." Ruth snapped off a salute. "Hail, Trojans," she said, and I laughed, too.

"Warden!" Mom cried. I clapped my hand over my mouth, as if the sound had come from me.

"What's that?" Ruth said. "I mean, who?"

"Nothing. No one. I've got to go," I said.

I tried to push the door closed, but Ruth wouldn't move her foot. I looked at her without blinking, even as I pushed harder on the door, pushed harder and harder against her foot, until finally Ruth yelped and yanked her foot free.

I slammed the door and ran to call Mrs. Ford. When I hung up the phone, the driveway was empty. Ruth was gone. I didn't have time to feel sad or happy about this; Mrs. Ford was already charging across our front yard, wearing dripping yellow dishwashing gloves and carrying her nurse's bag. A red bandana covered her short, coppery hair. She let herself into the house, tugged off her gloves, dropped them on the entryway floor, and strode to the living room. She smoothed Mom's hair and checked her pulse. Then she pulled a syringe and needle from her bag. I looked away as she slid the needle into Mom's thigh.

It took only a few minutes for the morphine to work its magic. Mom was gone again, where no one could reach her. Not even Dad. I was standing beside Mrs. Ford, looking down at Mom so still, when he appeared out of nowhere, his face floating like a pale balloon in the shadows of the living-room doorway.

"Thanks, Sharon," he said gruffly. "We're all right now."

"Are you sure?" Mrs. Ford waited, but Dad didn't answer. He was leaning over Mom now. He put his ear to her mouth, listened for her breathing. Mrs. Ford cleared her throat. "Do you want me to stay, Ward?"

"What?" Dad looked up, startled. He tried to smile. "You're still here? Don't you have a life?" He stretched his smile wider. "We're fine, Sharon. Seriously. We need rest, that's all."

Mrs. Ford looked at him.

"Did I say thanks? Thanks." Dad tucked the sheet more securely around Mom's shoulders.

At that, Mrs. Ford gave me a hug, and left as quickly as she'd come. For a moment, the house was so quiet it might as well have been empty. Then Dad sat down care-fully on the bed and drew his legs up beside Mom's. He was going to lie down beside her. He'd forgotten I was there.

"She woke up," I said loudly, like this was Dad's fault.

"Hush," he hissed. A moment passed, while he watched Mom. When she didn't stir, he said quietly, "You woke her?"

"No." I stomped my foot. I couldn't help it.

"Then what happened?" Dad said. "This shouldn't have happened."

"Warden," Mom murmured from her dreams.

"I'm here." Dad touched Mom's cheek, and then he turned to me. His expression was blank, as if he were looking at nothing—or something that might as well be nothing.

"If you can't take care of her, Livy, at least take care of yourself." Dad spoke softly, but I took a step back.

"What do you think I've been doing for the last year?" I tried to laugh. I sounded like I was choking.

"Well, try a little harder. Just try and keep a low profile. There's two of you and one of me, and Mom's the one of all of us who matters. Please."

"Please," Mom groaned in her sleep.

Remember your manners, Mom and Dad used to say when I was little. We like it when you say please. It makes it easier for us to help you.

I went to my room. "Please," I said, testing the empty air. I closed the door, but there was no need to lock it. No one was coming in.

JULY 3

The blackness is so thick, it almost seems to have substance. From far away comes the sound of feet, marching. I hope they're Mom's feet, but I don't think so. Mom never marches; Mom *strolls*. More feet join these feet. They're coming closer, getting louder. More feet and more, until it sounds like an army is approaching, an army so loud it feels like it's inside my head—*bang, bang, bang*. The army marches around me, kicks against me, leaps over me, and lands on the other side, almost hurting me, but not quite. Then it fades into the distance, the sound growing softer, the army getting smaller. Until there are two feet that aren't Mom's, marching away, gone altogether, leaving me alone in the dark.

I awoke from this dream at exactly ten minutes after midnight. It's almost one in the morning now. Outside, thunder booms. Rain falls in sheets, slapping up against my bedroom window and sweeping across the roof. But at least I'm not shivering so much anymore. When the dream woke me, I couldn't stop shaking. I stumbled to the bathroom to take my temperature, and dropped the thermometer on the floor. The back snapped off and the batteries fell out. I spent a long, hazy time trying to put the batteries back into the thermometer the right way. Pluses and minuses. Positive meets negative. Finally I stood and looked at myself in the mirror. Sweat trickled down my face. *Will you at least take care of yourself, Livy?* I wheeled around, but Dad wasn't there. I got a washcloth, wet it with cold water, and put it on my forehead like Mom used to do when I was sick.

The next thing I knew, I was in the kitchen, holding the phone to my ear. I'd dialed a number, and it was ringing.

"Hey," someone answered, like she'd been expecting me.

Ruth. I'd called Ruth.

"Hi." I pressed the cold washcloth to my eyes. "It's me."

"You who?" Ruth caught her breath. "Livy? Is that you?"

"Of course it's me."

"Of course?"

I heard something creak—the door to Ruth's

bedroom as she drew it closed. She had picked up the old, funky phone in the hallway. Its long cord, stretched to the limit, could extend to the green beanbag chair beside her bed. The chair rustled as Ruth settled into it.

"I leave messages for you all the time, but when was the last time you called me?" she said. "Let alone at this time of night. You're not exactly in my 'of course' category anymore."

"Oh." I clenched my teeth to keep them from chattering. "Anyway, what are you doing?"

"Waiting for the phone to ring, actually. I'm expecting another call." Ruth paused. "You're not checking up on me are you? I don't need two moms."

I do, I thought. I started to cry.

"Livy?"

I wasn't making a sound, I was sure of it. I pressed the washcloth against my mouth.

"Livy, are you okay?"

"Yes," I croaked.

"Stop bullshitting me. Stop with the bullshit."

I stopped crying. Since when did Ruth talk so tough?

"You've been pulling this secretive crap for too long, Livy, and I'm sick of it. Goddamn it, you didn't even send me a birthday card on my sixteenth birthday. You didn't even *say* happy birthday, and I passed you three times in the hall." Ruth wasn't whispering now; she was biting out the words. "Some blood sister you are."

May first. That's Ruth's birthday. It's also our blood sister anniversary. We've been blood sisters for ten years now that I think about it—ever since Ruth's sixth birthday party, when I first climbed up into her tree house. Pastor Bob had just built it, but not very well, it turned out. When Ruth told me I was the only friend she would allow inside, I jumped up in excitement, and my right leg crashed through a weak board. At first I didn't feel anything. But then I looked down and saw a long, jagged sliver of wood sticking out of my leg. There was blood, lots of it. And it hurt. "Help," I said to Ruth, whose face looked very pale. I spoke slowly and clearly to make sure she understood.

She understood. In a moment, she would run to find Pastor Bob, who would drive me to the emergency room. But first, she had to rub my blood onto her own leg and say, "We're blood sisters." I couldn't have cared less then. It was only the next day, when my stitches won me some attention at kindergarten, that I began to think about what Ruth had said. For a long time afterward, whenever I felt really alone, I traced the scar on my leg. I traced it again tonight.

"Help," I mumbled.

"What? I can't hear you."

The scar still felt a little tender.

"Help me." I spoke slowly and clearly to make sure she understood.

"Well, it's about time you asked." Ruth slammed the phone against something hard; the sound exploded in my ear.

"Hey," I yelped.

"You're just lucky you're not here." Ruth sounded like she was half serious. "Or that would have been you."

"It might as well have been."

"You're nuts, Livy. Certifiably nuts, do you know that? Who do you think you're fooling, anyway? I've known about your mom from the start. My mom told me right after her first surgery, but she said your parents had sworn her to secrecy, and that I had to promise never to talk about it with a soul, least of all you. I figured you'd tell me, so at first it wasn't a problem. Then weeks went by and I started to get mad. Well, it's been months now. It's about time you came to me."

"For help."

"For help, goddamn it."

"Which I am. Right now." But things didn't seem so bad anymore. I was still hot, maybe feverish, but I felt giddy, too. "Goddamn it, Ruth," I said, laughing, "hasn't your daddy told you that swearing is a sin?"

Ruth sighed wearily. "Like I said, Livy, I don't need two moms, and I definitely don't need two dads."

"I should go." I held the washcloth to my face. It felt clammy against my skin.

"Wait," Ruth said. "Wait. I miss you."

This time, that was all it took. I was crying again. I sounded like a baby.

"It's okay. It'll be okay." Ruth's voice broke. Was she crying, too?

Then came the click.

"Livy. Listen. That's probably my other call." Ruth sighed shakily. "I really have to get it. I've been waiting—"

I nodded into the washcloth. "I need to go to bed anyway."

"It'll be okay," Ruth said again, but firmly this time, like she was convinced. "I'll stop by your house tomorrow, four o'clock sharp. You'd better be ready."

"Thanks." I took a deep breath. "Blood Sister."

But Ruth had already hung up.

JULY 3

Dancing under water. A lonely waltz in the seaweed, a tangled turn and spin. Someone dips me deeply. In a rush of bubbles, I go down.

*F*our o'clock sharp was still an hour away. Mom was sleeping; Dad was watching her sleep. The house was too quiet, so I grabbed *Gone with the Wind* and slipped out to the backyard. There were blackbirds in the willow tree, making a racket; I wanted to be in the thick of all that noise. I carried a lawn chair over and sat down in the shade. I still felt woozy from the previous night and all the aspirin I'd popped since, but I opened my book anyway. The words blurred on the page. I looked up at the willow's long, swaying branches. When I was little I played my most private games beneath this tree. The branches became velvet curtains, waterfalls, and fortress walls. I pretended they concealed me completely; though, as I fought invisible enemies and danced with invisible partners, I often caught Mom watching me from the kitchen window. Sometimes she came and sat with me beneath the willow. We had our first picnics there.

Now I saw that the tree's leaves were yellow, not green, as if autumn had already arrived. The willow is dying, nearly dead, according to Dad. He's going to cut it down. Before it spreads its disease to other trees, he'll dig it out and chop it to bits. And there's another reason our willow has to go: according to Dad, we planted it too close to the house. Before long, the roots will crack the foundation or entangle themselves in water lines, and cause more damage than the tree is worth. Last spring, Dad said the tree was nothing but a weed, which made Mom mad enough to slam her glass down on the kitchen counter and say, "Is it that easy for you to let things go?"

That was the last time I heard her raise her voice to him—not that she ever did it that often before. Now when she speaks, she sounds not much louder than the wind that was suddenly whispering through the willow's branches.

Four o'clock sharp was maybe forty-five minutes away now. And counting. Yellow leaves drifted down on me, and I closed my eyes. The leaves touched my skin like gentle fingers.

The next thing I knew, there was something over my head, something rough and thick—burlap, it felt like. "Dad!" I screamed, but he didn't come running.

Strange hands were on me, holding me down. I started hitting. I tumbled from the chair to the ground and rolled in the grass, but the hands grabbed me. "One, two, three," a guy said, and I was lifted clumsily into the air. "She's heavier than she looks," another guy said. Their voices were familiar. These were kids from school.

"Surprise, Livy!" Ruth's voice, way too cheery. "Four o'clock came and went. I've been waiting at your front door for at least ten minutes."

"You wouldn't want to keep anyone waiting," yet another guy said.

"Let me go!" I hollered through the burlap. Whoever was out there just laughed, then began dragging me across the yard. When my back scraped the driveway, I kicked and made contact. "Shit," Ruth said, "we're *rescuing* you!" I kicked harder. The laughter stopped.

"Are you sure this is a good idea?" Ruth's voice quavered.

"You wouldn't know fun if it whacked you over the head, would you, Ruthie?" said one of the guys.

Someone cinched my hands behind my back with what felt like a leather belt.

"Yes, I would!"

Keys jangled and a door screeched open on rusty hinges.

"No!" I yelled. My stomach lurched as they pushed me into the car. The skin on the back of my thighs stuck and squeaked against hot vinyl.

"Don't suffocate her," a girl said. Not Ruth.

But no one yanked the bag from my head. I sucked in a close, dusty breath and coughed, spitting out strands of burlap. The car heaved as warm bodies pressed up against me. Doors slammed. Then the engine revved, and we tore out of the driveway and away.

The car jolted over bumps and swung around corners and curves. I leaned up against some guy's brawny shoulder, then a skinny arm I recognized as Ruth's. With my hands twisted behind me, there was nothing to hold on to. Stereo speakers thudded at my head.

Finally the car made a sharp right turn and lurched to a stop. A door opened and the brawny guy bolted, jouncing the seat. I fell into the space where he had been, and Ruth laughed. She pulled me out of the car. Someone finally yanked off the bag, the belt. Everything spun in a swirl of color. I couldn't move; I could barely stand. I could definitely vomit. So I did.

Luckily, I vomited outside the car. Unluckily for someone, I vomited on a pair of leather Adidas, white with green racing stripes. Covered now with my pink puke. The shoes danced around like they could dance themselves clean. "Yuck," the shoes' owner said, scraping his Adidas across the grass. "Fuckin' yuck."

I wiped my arm across my nose and mouth, and looked up to see Gil Perez, football player extraordinaire, slapping his strong, brown hands against his thighs as he danced. *Gil Perez.* I stared at him in shock. A football player wouldn't kidnap Coach's Daughter. For starters, he wouldn't want to piss off Coach. And, bottom line, Coach's Daughter doesn't merit that kind of effort.

Then it dawned on me that Gil is probably the only football player who would kidnap Coach's Daughter (me), because Coach (Dad) would never get angry with Gil. Gil is Dad's favorite Trojan, and everybody at Troy City High knows it. Gil is the leader of the Jock Herd, the football team's Most Valuable Player, Dad's shadow and champion. Or Gil was all these things last year. Then he graduated with the rest of the senior class, a green-and-gold tassel swinging from his mortarboard. "Enough of this white-bread town!" Gil yelled, as the ceremony finished. "I'm out of here!" He was the first to throw his mortarboard into the air.

You can't take your eyes off Gil, whether he is catching a football, crossing a room, or dancing on Chloe Cunningham's front lawn, which is what he was doing at the moment. This was how Ruth had decided to help me, by taking me to a float-making party. Her vision; my nightmare. I looked at Ruth, but she seemed to have forgotten everything but Gil. She was gazing dreamily at him; something about her expression made me feel like I might vomit again. I groaned. Ruth must have heard, because she glanced my way.

"Oh God, Livy." She gave me a rueful smile. "Are you okay? This was supposed to be fun."

"Yeah." Gil kicked off his shoes. "Great way to spend an afternoon, Jackie."

"Aw, poor little Gil." Jackie Perez, Gil's younger sister, sauntered around the car to stand beside Ruth. "Should we lick those clean for you?"

Gil glared at Jackie. "On your knees."

"Dream on," she said.

I said Dad would do anything for Gil—well, Gil would do that and more for Jackie. I guess he would even drive her and her good friend—Ruth, apparently, from

the way they kept whispering to each other now—
to a party for ex-sophomores. After all, Gil took Jackie to
his senior prom, and though every cheerleader lamented
this fact, no one dared make fun of them. Jackie is as
intimidating as Gil, in her own way. Like Ruth and me,
she's never been a part of a Herd. "Screw Herds," she'd
probably say, if she happened to notice their existence.
Jackie seems to care only about grades, and she makes
straight A's. She stands tall, holds her head high, and sits
in the front row of every class. She keeps her long black
hair up in a bun. With her perfect posture and slender
neck, she reminds me of someone from the nineteenth
century—a novelist, maybe, or a high-society lady. Even
when she swears, she sounds elegant, like she's quoting
poetry.

Case in point: When Gil continued to sulk, Jackie
snatched up his Adidas, flung them into the bushes,
and said, "Forget the fucking shoes. The pizza is getting
cold."

"Shit, yeah," Ruth said brightly. "I'm hungry. Okay,
Gil?"

When Gil didn't look at Ruth, let alone answer her,
she turned to me. "Okay, Livy?"

Ruth was acting like a different person—like Jackie,
I realized. Except she didn't have Jackie's flair for, well,

being Jackie. Ruth looked like a different person, too, I noticed now. For the first time in years, her hair was short. It lay in a cap of curls around her head, tight ringlets that trailed off into tendrils.

"Nice do," I said.

"You like?" Ruth batted her lashes. Then she glanced at Gil. "Come on, Livy, let's go, already. Have some fun."

"Oh, I *have* been having fun." I swallowed the sour taste in my mouth and nearly gagged. "A super time."

"Um, guys?" A hesitant voice came from behind me.

"'Um, guys?'" Another voice, sarcastically mimicking the first. I turned to see Ed Allen and Charlie Wates.

Charlie is a soon-to-be senior, running back, and Gil's close comrade. Next year, Charlie might replace Gil as Dad's shadow and champion—if Charlie gets more disciplined. Dad says that Charlie's got potential, but he's also got too much attitude for his own good. Freshman year Charlie told Dad to "shove it" at football practice, and Dad kicked him off the team for the rest of the season. Charlie must have spent two years making it up to Dad, because he played first-string last year.

Charlie lifeguards in the summer, and he gets so tan that his skin fades to a color that can only be described as yellow by winter. He has a great tan now, though. And his shiny, blond hair is long; his bangs nearly hide his green eyes. Come football season, Dad will make Charlie shave his head, probably.

Charlie and Gil are inseparable; where one is, you expect to see the other—kind of like Ruth and I used to be. But I was surprised to see Ed Allen. Like Charlie, Ed is going to be a senior next year. Ed plays football, too, but Ed is always on the bench. He's a little goofy; there's no other way to put it. The only time I ever saw Ed approach Gil or Charlie was once during a game, when he dared to bring them water bottles. He stood at the outskirts of the huddle, his sandy hair untouched by a football helmet, still perfectly styled, spiked with gel. Ed waited there until the last minute, then he gave water bottles to Charlie and Gil, who took them without so much as a thank-you. But I guess that's the reason why Ed's presence shouldn't have surprised me, after all. Why wouldn't Gil and Charlie want a willing servant hanging around?

"Um, guys?" Ed said again. He has a habit of speaking in questions even when he's making a statement. "Shouldn't we be heading up to the party? While the beer's still flowing? It's a real drag when a keg goes dry?"

"Cool it," said Gil.

Charlie said, "Stop salivating."

But Gil was the one who might as well have been salivating, the way he was staring up the hill at Chloe's barn. Still staring, he went over to Ruth and slung his arm over her shoulder. He leaned into her, like she was a wall or a prop. Ruth bit her lip and twirled one of her tendrils.

"Ahem." Jackie rapped her knuckles against the car's roof. "Ed is right. The party calls."

Charlie laughed. "Actually, it looks like we're getting a personal invitation."

That's when I saw Chloe Cunningham coming down the hill toward us, her toned legs and arms swinging easily with each stride.

"Hey, Gil, I've been waiting for you." Chloe stopped short. "Well, if it isn't Saint Ruth."

"Ruth's got a bad case of halo-head, that's for sure." Gil ruffled Ruth's hair and sauntered over to Chloe. He wrapped his arm around Chloe's waist and pulled her close.

"Ah!" Chloe sighed. "You're barefoot. My, what tan feet you have!"

"The better to dance with you, my dear," Gil said with a growl.

"It's called brown skin, Chloe," Jackie said. "We're

46

spics, Gil and me, remember? I've heard rumors that your family is really into racial issues and stuff. Like, you're not afraid to run your opinions up the flagpole." Jackie jerked her thumb at Chloe's house. Sure enough, there was a Confederate flag billowing right below the Stars and Stripes.

"So my parents are from Alabama. So what?" Chloe kicked off her shoes and wiggled her toes in the grass. "Mmm. Bare feet are the best."

Jackie jumped on the car's hood and crossed one leg over the other with an exasperated sigh.

"Ignore her," Gil said to Chloe.

"It's the riffraff." Chloe nodded at Ruth and me. "Don't you know they're a bad influence on your little sister? Come on, let's go."

Chloe's wavy brown hair flicked from side to side as she turned and loped off toward the barn, and her pink gauzy shirt drifted against her body. Guys always say that Chloe has the perfect figure. She wears short shorts (every chance she gets); just then she seemed the human equivalent of Barbie, only softer and warmer.

Ruth refused to watch Gil and Chloe walk up the hill.

"Don't let Chloe get to you, gals," Charlie said. "She's hot, sure. But, hey, she also throws a great party."

Charlie jogged after Gil, and Ed said, "Wait?" and jogged after Charlie. Then Ruth yanked Jackie from the car, grabbed my hand, and dragged us toward the barn. My heart was pounding suddenly, and it wasn't from running. I hadn't been to a dance since seventh grade, when I spent the entire two hours standing by the punch bowl with Ruth. We kept our backs to the dance floor, as if we couldn't have cared less what was going on there.

As if.

At the barn's wide doorway, Ruth, Jackie, and I paused to get our bearings. Techno throbbed from a stereo. There wasn't a punch bowl in sight. There was a keg, though, and maybe ten couples dancing in a way that made my cheeks go warm. Another large group of kids stood by a table littered with open pizza boxes, bags of chips, bottles of soda. Those kids were eating as if they were ravenous, stealing nervous glances at the dancers all the while.

Jackie headed directly for the food table. That left Ruth and me standing in the shadows.

I looked at her. "Feels like old times."

Ruth smiled, but she didn't look happy. She was searching the barn for someone, and I wasn't surprised when her eyes settled on Gil. He was sitting on a hay bale, devouring a handful of chips. Chloe sat beside him, one arm draped over his shoulders.

"So," I said quickly, because now Ruth looked like she might cry. "Since when did you like parties?" As far as I knew, she hadn't been to a dance since seventh grade, either.

"Since Jackie."

"Oh." I leaned against the barn's rough wood wall, trying to look casual.

Ruth gave a shaky sigh.

"Jackie is cool. And since I'm her friend, people think I'm cool, too. So parties are cool."

"Cool," I said.

With the toe of her sandal, Ruth drew a line on the dusty floor. "Listen, Livy. There are some decent people here."

"People like Gil?" I said. Maybe I was sneering just a little bit.

"No, people like Gil's sister." Ruth frowned, irritated. "But check back in a month or so, and see if anything has changed. It was Gil on the phone last night, you know. I was waiting for him to call. He wanted to ask me about Jackie's birthday. It's in a few weeks. He knows I know what kind of present she really wants." Ruth glanced at the hay bales, but Gil was nowhere to be seen.

Suddenly, I felt bad for Ruth. The way I did when Chloe called her a saint—when anyone did her wrong in any way. So I said, "Having a new friend has a lot of perks, I guess."

Ruth studied me for a moment. Then she smiled and said, "I think you and Jackie would have a lot in common, if you'd give her a chance."

"Me? Give *Jackie* a chance?"

"She'll give you a chance, too. Especially if you're just yourself, like I was when we met. She can be really sweet, Livy. One day last spring, I wore my white jeans to school, and of course, I got my period in a big way, right in the middle of math class. I was about ready to die, when Jackie somehow got me to the bathroom and gave me a tampon and her gym shorts."

"Wow," I said lamely.

Ruth shrugged. "Jackie told me that she'd always liked the fact that I was smart, that I asked interesting questions in class. She'd wanted to get to know me, she said, since this one English class when I'd asked if we could read stories by people other than white guys. She appreciated that, being Mexican and all. Anyway." Ruth linked her arm through mine. "I missed you, see? I was just lucky that Jackie was around to keep me company, and lucky that she kept such fun company herself."

Ruth was dancing beside me now, mimicking the movements of the girl who was dancing with Ed—a girl who skulks around school like a shadow, who turned out to be amazing on the dance floor. Ed wasn't a bad dancer, either. In fact, he was kind of good. He was smiling like he was truly enjoying himself, and, unlike the other guys, he was actually looking at the shadow girl, catching her around the waist or by the hand at just the right moment.

"Now, that's the place to be." Ruth nodded toward the hayloft, where Jackie and Charlie sat with a few other kids, dangling their legs over the edge. She nudged me in the ribs. "Let's go up. The altitude will do you good."

I didn't want to be left alone, so I followed Ruth up the ladder into the hayloft and sat down by Jackie and Charlie. For a while, we simply watched the dancers. Ruth clutched my arm when Chloe and Gil appeared from behind some hay bales and quickly took over the center of the floor. Chloe, who you would think would be a great dancer, couldn't seem to find the beat. Gil danced like he was born doing it, with a style that was completely his own. He worked his way around the floor like a cat, slinking in perfect time to the music, though he kept touching base with Chloe, not looking at her exactly, just prowling by, rubbing against her. Compared to Gil, Ed, and the shadow girl, the other kids looked like

"Are you familiar with that stuff?" she said.

"Sure." I drank again. I could barely swallow that mouthful, so I swallowed some more to wash it down. Last night's fever seemed to have returned. I looked at the bodies shifting around on the dance floor. Suddenly everyone there seemed to be moving together in some kind of complicated pattern, like they'd been choreographed. I didn't know the routine. I drank again.

"You've got your father's backbone, that's for sure." Charlie's voice held a hint of admiration. Then his voice softened, like butter melting. "I really respect your father, by the way. You can feel free to tell him that."

"Just so you know," Jackie said, "I got looped on Boone's Farm once, only once, and it wasn't pretty. Never again, I swore, on *my* father's honor."

"Here's to your father, long may he reign," I toasted and took a big gulp. "Here's to all our fathers."

"May they never be a pain," Ruth chimed in, "like mine is." She yanked the bottle away.

"Hey. No grabbing." I grinned at Ruth, then at Jackie, but Jackie didn't smile back.

"Don't ever joke about my father," she said, "ever again."

I grabbed the bottle back from Ruth. "What's that supposed to mean?" My words didn't come out too clearly.

53

Jackie said, "It means go ahead and drink yourself sick."

"Come on, Livy." Charlie snapped his fingers in front of my face. "Don't hog the hooch."

"What am I saying? You're already sick, all of you." Jackie stomped across the hayloft and climbed down the ladder.

"Christ, Livy." Ruth groaned. "Now you've done it."

"Me?" I stammered. "What . . . why?"

But Ruth was already following Jackie down the ladder.

I stole a glance at Charlie. With Jackie and Ruth gone, I wasn't sure he would give me the time of day. But he was studying me carefully, like I was a biological specimen he'd never seen before. When he saw me looking at him, he shook his hair from his green eyes and flashed a smile. I grinned back like an idiot, but I couldn't think of anything to say. It can be awfully quiet between two people, even when music is making the world shake around you. I bit my lip until it hurt, searching my brain for a topic.

"I didn't mean to freak Jackie out." My voice came out in an apologetic croak.

"Don't worry about it." Charlie closed his eyes for a moment. When he opened them again, they seemed more bloodshot than before. "Jackie is thin-skinned about certain things. Well, about one thing in particular—her family."

"But what did I say?" Now I sounded whiny.

"It's no big deal. Give me that, will you?"

I passed the bottle to Charlie. He tipped it back and drained it.

"I didn't mean to hurt anyone's feelings." I winced. Just shut up, I thought. *Shut up.*

Charlie licked his lips. "Sure, whatever. I mean, how could you know? She and Gil don't exactly make it public knowledge."

I waited for clarification.

"You got a great mouth, anybody ever tell you that?" Charlie shook his hair back again. "You're kind of a babe, actually."

"Um," I stammered. "Everyone in my family says I've got my dad's mouth."

Great.

"Well, yeah." Charlie shrugged. "Only, your mouth is softer and it doesn't tell me what to do, where to get off."

I wanted to feel offended, not flattered. But I felt myself grinning again. "Anyway," I said quickly. "What's up with Jackie?"

"Oh, her dad died a few years back. Gil's freshman year, I think, so she would have been just a kid. They've only got their mom now, who works two jobs, so they never see her. Basically that means they've only got each other. So that's why they're thin-skinned when it comes to family stuff." Charlie scooted closer to me. "End of story."

"Oh." The barn was tilting at a crazy angle—toward Charlie.

"Here." He passed me a can of beer. He seemed to have produced it out of thin air. "Hair of the dog."

"I thought 'hair of the dog' was for the morning after," I said. But I drank deeply. The beer tasted cold and clean after the Boone's Farm; so cold and clean it couldn't do me harm. I finished the can.

Next I remember a blur of bottles and cans, and the taste of rotting strawberries in my mouth. Then somehow, I was down the ladder and on the dance floor, holding Charlie's hand—holding his hand for a moment, maybe, before I started to dance. Because when I started to dance, Charlie seemed to vanish. I might as well have been up in my bedroom, pretending to be a Southern belle at a ball. I was dancing, gliding, twirling around. All by myself. No Charlie, no Ruth, no crowded barn, no Dad, no Mom. In time, but completely out of it.

At one point, I opened my eyes—I hadn't realized they were closed—and saw that a space had been cleared for me. Kids were standing in a ring around me, watching. I couldn't tell anything from their expressions. I was moving too fast, for one thing. Then I whirled past Ruth, and she came into focus. She was standing close to Jackie, and both of them were smiling slightly, not *with* me but *at* me, which is another thing altogether. Their smiles made me realize just how hard I was dancing. I was dancing like my body was the place I felt most free, like I was celebrating *it*, not our country's birthday or a parade float. I took a few stumbling steps, then stood stock still, right in front of the battering ram. Ruth was right. The float did look real enough to do some damage.

I took a step back. My stomach churned, and I dripped with sweat. Except for the thudding music, the barn was quiet. The few kids still dancing slowed to watch me, and suddenly it looked like they were moving under water. The music came at me that way too; or like someone was playing a record on the wrong speed.

"Wow," a guy said, his voice dripping with sarcasm. "Some solo, Olive Oyl."

A girl laughed. "I couldn't keep up with her if I tried."

The guy standing next to her slapped her butt. "Don't you dare try."

Everyone laughed at that, and I wanted to hide in a corner. The only problem was, I couldn't move.

Chloe said, "I guess I should have hired a bouncer." Her laughter sounded sharp as icicles breaking. "Someone to keep things under control."

Ruth stepped forward. She put her arm around my shoulder. "Nice footwork," she whispered. And then Jackie was there too, not looking at me, but there.

"You got some control issues, Chloe?" Jackie said. "I mean, what are you going for here, a Hitler Youth kind of a thing? 'Dance like this, walk like this, look like this, be like this—or you're outta here.' Scary implications, if you ask me. Right, Gil?"

Gil shifted back and forth on his bare feet.

"You sound like Miss Affirmative Action, or something." Chloe punched her fist in the air. "Equal rights for all dancers, without regard for ability!"

Gil looked at Jackie for a long moment. Then he turned to Chloe and said, "I think I need some fresh air." And he walked out of the barn.

Ruth and Jackie steered me outside, too. We'd just caught up to Gil when I stumbled, and strawberry syrup rose up in my throat.

"Oh no," I groaned.

"Don't let her trash the place." Chloe—a shapely black silhouette surrounded by harsh light—had followed us to the barn's doorway.

Gil shied away from me. "Not on me you don't!" he yelped, and he pushed me toward some bushes. I buried my face in their cool, smooth leaves. I managed to swallow what was inside me. Hands settled on my shoulders as I quieted. The warm weight of them calmed me.

"You okay?" Ruth's voice. Ruth's hands.

I turned slowly on wobbly legs. Ruth's smile, clear even in the shadows, sweet and sad and sorry for me. Tears stung my eyes. With her fingertips, Ruth brushed them away.

"Come on, you party animal, you."

I followed her down the driveway to Gil's car. Jackie fell into step beside me.

"Thanks," Jackie said.

"For what?" My voice was husky.

"For helping my brother ditch that chick. He's been hooked on Chloe for maybe two months now. It feels like a year. I've been trying to tell him what a hypocrite she is. If he weren't such a jock, she wouldn't want to touch him with her big toe. As it is, we're honorary white folks

59

in her book. Gil has always known her deal. He just let his testosterone get in the way of his brain."

I thought: here is a person whose father has died. She is walking beside me now, cool, calm, and collected; she is guiding me along. I opened my mouth to ask Jackie something—How did you do it? How did you survive? Did you ever think you wouldn't?—I wasn't sure what. But then we were at the car. Gil was already sitting behind the steering wheel. Jackie jumped into the front seat beside him, and Ed followed her. Ruth got into the backseat. I stood with my hand on the door, trying to catch my balance so I could slide in without falling over.

"Need some help?"

For the second time, Charlie's voice made me jump. I hadn't realized he was standing right behind me. He put his hands on my hips and pushed me into the backseat. Then he sat down beside me.

I tried to stay awake. I tried to listen to Ed jabbering on about who would stand where on the floats tomorrow. I tried to watch the road and see where we were going. But I felt like a towel, wrung out and hung to dry, limp and damp, and not at all clean. At one point, Gil pinched his nose and said that I stank. But I was too tired to care. I merely said, "Thank you, thank you very much," which made everyone laugh. We turned a corner, and I fell against

Charlie. I couldn't lift my head from his shoulder. I let my eyes close. I dreamed of dancing under water. When I woke again, Charlie was pulling me out of the car and leading me into darkness.

"Where have I been?" My tongue felt swollen. "Where am I?"

"Around." Charlie grinned slyly. "Now you're home."

Somehow we were standing on my front porch. There wasn't a light on anywhere in the house. I turned away from Charlie so he wouldn't smell my breath. "Thanks for getting me here."

"No problem. It's on the way."

"On the way where?"

"To whatever's next."

"Well, thanks again," I said to his back as he walked away. Far away, fireworks boomed. The fire department was testing things out for tomorrow's show, or else a kid was messing around, blinding himself, probably. I crept into the house. I was definitely sober now, with a fierce headache, like someone had whacked an ax right into my forehead. Dad must have been wiped out, too, because neither he nor Mom stirred as I crept past them, lying together on the hospital bed in the living room. What with no lecture, no note, no nothing, Dad probably hadn't even noticed I was gone. If he had noticed, he would probably forget by morning.

Maybe I'd have forgotten, too, if I hadn't pulled out this journal.

JULY 4

Brush your teeth! Use mouthwash, soap, lye, if you have to! Get rid of that taste!

My body might as well be a sandbag cemented to the bed. So I can't obey the strange, scolding voice that is mine.

When I cracked my eyes this morning, I still had that awful taste in my mouth, and Mrs. Ford was standing over me in her nurse's uniform. I felt so sick to my stomach that, for a moment, I thought she was there for me, not Mom. My headache was so bad, I couldn't imagine getting out of bed. I shivered and pulled the sheet over my head.

"There's a car full of kids waiting for you out front." Mrs. Ford's voice seemed louder than usual. "They keep revving the engine like they've got somewhere important to go. If it's the parade, you'd better hurry up or you'll miss it. Your dad left a long time ago."

"But—" I peeked over the edge of the sheet. "Mom?"

"I'll stay with her." Mrs. Ford smiled as she turned to go back downstairs. "You have some fun. For once."

I got up as quickly as I could, threw on some clothes, then went to the bathroom. I did all the basic things I usually do and can accomplish in about three minutes. Plus, I did something extra: I rummaged through the messy drawer that was Mom's, through hairbrushes and combs that held strands of brown hair, not gray; through half-used tubes of clumpy mascara and candy-colored lipsticks. Finally I found the lipstick I was looking for—a soft peach shade that she let me wear to a wedding last year. I slicked some on my lips. It looked sloppy at the corners, not sleek like before, when Mom helped apply it. But the peach color still brightened my face.

I looked into the mirror, into my eyes. "Hello," I practiced. "Hi."

The lipstick made my mouth look like someone else's mouth. Not Dad's, the way I told Charlie last night, but Mom's. My mouth looked like Mom's when she was young and healthy. I lifted a Kleenex to wipe off the lipstick, then didn't. Instead, I went quietly downstairs and out the front door. I was careful not to look at the hospital bed in the living room. "Bye," I whispered as the door closed behind me. I held on to the handle. I shouldn't be wearing her lipstick, I thought. I should be with her, watching parades on TV.

But there was the green sedan waiting in the driveway, with Gil and Jackie in the front seat, and Ruth and Charlie in the backseat. Apparently Chloe *was* history. I walked slowly to the car.

Ruth leaned out the window and grinned. "What took you so long? Get in quick. We want to get a good spot to see the parade."

I tried not to stare at Charlie. Suddenly, my face and hands were clammy. I couldn't get sick again. Not two times in less than twenty-four hours. Not in public.

"I don't think I can go," I said.

Ruth slapped her hand against the car door. "What do you mean? You *have* to go."

"I *have* to help my mom. We have things we have to do today."

"Please?" Charlie got out of the car and ambled over to me. He looked past me at the house. "Your dad's already gone, right? I mean, if he's still here I could let him know we're giving you a ride."

I ducked my head, flustered. "He's gone."

"Okay. Whatever." Charlie tipped up my chin so that I had to meet his eyes. He winked at me. "Get a move on, then. Pretty please?"

I couldn't help but smile. What the heck, I thought. Mom was probably sleeping anyway. I let a shrug be my answer, but Charlie still made a big show of being gallant. Bowing and sweeping his arm wide, he directed me to the car. I started to laugh, then couldn't stop laughing. I was on the verge of hysteria by the time I was sitting in the backseat between Charlie and Ruth, who rolled her eyes at me. I couldn't believe a guy—let alone Charlie Wates—was making me feel like Scarlett O'Hara from *Gone with the Wind*.

"Calm down," Jackie said. "You'll piss your pants."

That calmed me right down. I sank low in the seat, embarrassed into silence. Charlie sank down beside me, almost touching me, but not quite. I sat very still, staring at our two legs so close together. If I did anything that he didn't like, he'd move away from me, I was sure.

We sped toward town. As Gil drove, he kept turning up the radio until the speakers vibrated and rattled. It was impossible to talk, and that was fine by me. I could concentrate on keeping my stomach calm; I could concentrate on not flinching every time Charlie's arm brushed against mine. When we were almost to town, I finally leaned over to Ruth and yelled, "What's the big hurry? It's just a parade, right?"

"You're really out of it," Ruth shouted back. "Don't you know the entire football team is riding on your dad's float today?"

I couldn't very well say: What float? My dad has a float?

"We'll just make it," Gil hollered, too close to Jackie's ear.

Jackie snapped off the radio. "Thanks, Gil. I'm totally deaf now."

"You've got to make it." Ruth wrapped her arms around Gil's headrest. "It is a big deal. Coach is expecting you. He told you that."

In the sudden silence, my ears felt stuffed with cotton. Plus, my headache was worse than ever. Coach, I thought dully. Dad. It's just like I thought: he tells people like Gil things that he'd never tell me.

"Hey, we've got his little girl here. We're late because of her." Charlie squeezed my knee, and I almost yelped. Then he took his hand away. "Coach can't hold us accountable if we're late because of her."

"He should thank you, if anything," Ruth said. "You've brought her out into the light of day."

Her, I thought. Livy. *Me*. I elbowed Ruth. Her face reddened, but she didn't apologize.

Gil swung the car into the library parking lot and cut the engine. Then he and Charlie were off and running, zigzagging between parked cars. Jackie and Ruth sprinted after them and so I followed, too, at a slower pace. We were three blocks from the parade route, but I could already see and hear people gathering along Main Street. I kept my breathing steady. That seemed to clear my head. At least I felt well enough to push my way through the crowd, past lawn chairs, coolers, and strollers to where Jackie and Ruth stood waiting at the curb. The judges' table was right beside us.

"Excellent maneuvering," Ruth said, as a whistle pierced the air.

"It's starting," Jackie said. "Put in your earplugs."

"What earplugs?" I said.

Ruth shook her head, smiling. "She's joking."

"I've never been more serious," Jackie said.

A moment later sirens blared, and when they didn't stop, we clapped our hands over our ears. Every police car, fire truck, and ambulance in the county was passing in front of us. The parade had officially begun, led by the mayor, sitting in a gold Cadillac convertible. Behind him were the Shriners, hunched like bulky bears in their kiddy cars, zipping this way and that, the tassels on their fezzes flying. Sheriff Byrne followed them, mounted on a black horse that pranced down Main Street in time with the Troy City High School Marching Band, which was playing "Yankee Doodle."

"Yeehaw! Ride 'em, Cowboy Byrne!" Ruth cheered, her voice rising above all the noise. Sheriff Byrne sat taller, pretending he hadn't heard.

The band was playing "America the Beautiful" now, as the freshman float rolled slowly past us—a giant Helen of Troy with big tissue-paper hair. Following in her shadow was our float. Ruth, Jackie, and I howled at the sight of Chloe astride the battering ram. She wore a toga and a wreath of silver leaves in her hair and silver sandals on her feet, and she sucked in her stomach and arched her back like the figurehead on the prow of a galleon, so that her breasts seemed to lead the way. "Is she even breathing?" Jackie wondered. Red-faced pep club members were pretending to heave the battering ram—and Chloe—into a fake brick wall. I hugged myself, the laughter felt so good. I didn't feel sick anymore, even as I watched the junior float wobble by—a Trojan ship bobbing crazily on a blue sea. Behind it came the senior float, a miniature Troy, the swaying towers and fortresses marked with the names of local businesses.

And then came Dad's float. I heard its fanfare first—our school song played by a solo trumpet. The music poured through the air like liquid gold. I looked for the trumpeter, but the float blocked my view. It was a yellow Trojan horse that stood at least fifteen feet high, its head level with the pots of red and white geraniums that swung from the tops of streetlamps. The horse's teeth looked dangerous; you could see the whites of its eyes. You didn't think *tissue paper*, taking it all in. The mane and tail were made of silky green cords, which ruffled in the wind; the massive, rigid legs anchored the horse firmly to an AstroTurf bed. Gil was sitting in the Trojan horse's saddle, giving cocky salutes to the cheering crowd. The rest of the football players and cheerleaders stood below him, including Charlie, who was clapping in time with the school song.

"Go, Gil!" Ruth yelled.

Jackie just beamed. I craned my neck to get a glimpse of Dad. He stood tall by the horse's head, the reins clenched in his hand. He was wearing his coach's uniform, a dark suit with a white shirt and a green-and-gold-striped tie. He had one foot propped on last year's trophy and his right hand over his heart. He leveled his gaze slightly above the crowd, at something nobody else could see, but his expression was so proud, so noble, it made me catch my breath. Whatever he saw above our heads made him seem like more than a coach or a father or a man. Dad seemed like a hero.

The float came to a stop in front of the judge's booth. Dad pulled the reins aside, and Ed Allen stepped forward.

"What's *Ed* doing there?" Ruth said.

Ed closed his eyes and lifted a trumpet to his lips. He took a deep breath. His fingers flashed on the valves. Notes darted high and low; music swelled and soared. Ed was taking the school song to surprising places. Jazz, I thought. That's what he was playing—stuff I'd heard only in passing, played on radio stations broadcast from Chicago.

"Incredible," I said.

Jackie nodded.

"Yeah, great float," Ruth said.

"That's not what I mean," I said. "Ed can really play."

"Oh, yeah, Ed," Ruth said vaguely, her eyes on Gil.

People started to sing along, and Ed adjusted his playing to become more like an accompaniment—but still a better accompaniment than any I'd heard:

> *Troy City Trojans*
> *Battling brave and true.*
> *Charging on toward victory*
> *In everything we do.*

Standing beside Ed, Dad smiled more radiantly than before. I wish Mom could see you now, I thought, my eyes stinging with sudden tears. Mom would be asleep in her bed, or clutching Mrs. Ford's hand. But Dad wasn't thinking about anything like morphine or bedpans or death. He was a hero now. He could do that, switch off and on parts of his life, and he'd taught me how to do it, too.

I couldn't look at him anymore. I looked at the streamers, confetti, and garbage littered at my feet.

"You're a great coach, Coach!" someone shouted.

"And a great husband, too!" hollered Ruth.

Dad whirled around and bumped into Ed, who almost dropped his trumpet. A murmur swept through the crowd. I stared at Ruth, too shocked to be mad. She should know what's public and what's private. She should know better.

Ruth lifted her shoulders. "I was trying to be encouraging. For both of your sakes."

"He didn't seem like he needed that much encouragement," Jackie said.

Ed started playing again, and the cheering quickly resumed. Dad found the reins and propped his foot back on the trophy, but he didn't look like he was seeing a vision anymore. He looked like he was staring at a wall.

The float rolled on toward the finish line. As Ed's music faded in the distance, the sad county-fair clowns ambled by. The parade was over.

"All righty, then." Ruth gave me a quick hug, trying to make things okay again. "Onward and upward. Time to get trashed, girls."

"Oh, yeah?" Pastor Bob had come up behind us. His bald head glistened with sweat. "What's that you say, sweetie?"

"Dad!" Ruth glanced at Jackie and me, then pursed her lips and gave Pastor Bob a worried look. "You got sunburned again."

Warily, he touched his scalp, which had turned an angry red. "I keep forgetting my hat." He sighed. "Never mind. Your mom's waiting in the car. We have to get to Uncle Will's, pronto."

Ruth groaned. "I forgot."

"I reminded you at breakfast this morning."

"*I forgot.* And besides, I have plans with Livy and Jackie." She bumped her hip against Jackie's. "*This* is Jackie, Dad. Straight A's, remember?"

"Hello." Jackie dutifully held out her hand, and Pastor Bob vigorously shook it.

"I've heard a lot about you, Ms. Perez, and I hope to get better acquainted soon. Until then, have a lovely Fourth. Without my daughter. Come on, hon."

"Dad," Ruth spoke through gritted teeth. "My plans."

"Plan on this: a family reunion at your Great-uncle Will's."

"Boring. I'll be the only one under thirty and over seven. And Will won't even notice if I'm there or not."

"Ruth. Whether or not you care that your great-uncle is very sick, I do." He looked quickly at me. "You'll excuse Ruth today, right, Livy? I know you two are long overdue for a visit, but you of all people understand what's important, I'm sure. We don't want to have any regrets. We spend time with those we love before it's too late, don't we?"

"We don't. I mean, we do. Sure." My mouth had gone so dry that my voice was raspy. I stretched my lips into a smile. Smiling, I croaked, "Boy, am I thirsty."

"Jesus, Dad," Ruth said. "Lighten up. Everything doesn't have to have a moral, with a capital M."

I caught my breath. Often enough, I'd heard Pastor Bob preach, "Don't use God's name in vain." But his gentle gray eyes didn't waver as he studied his daughter; his face stayed calm even as he said, "Baby, you just sealed your fate." Then bent low, scooped up Ruth, and tossed her over his shoulder like a sack of grain. Ruth wriggled

74

and twisted and begged Jackie and me to save her, but Pastor Bob started walking and he didn't break his stride.

"Whoa." Jackie watched in admiration as Pastor Bob and Ruth disappeared around the corner. "Reverend Tough Love."

"Tough break for Ruth." I shrugged, trying to shake it off. Forget Uncle Will. Forget Dad. Forget Mom. Forget.

Jackie frowned. "He's right, though. Ruth should go see her uncle."

"It's just hard, all the stuff she has to do because of her father."

"This isn't just about her father. It's *her* uncle."

"What if she went and saw her uncle another day? What's so wrong with that?"

"Well—"

"That's the problem with Ruth's father. He's nice, and everything, but he's always so sure he's right. He doesn't listen to Ruth, and that bugs her. I know. She's told me. For years," I couldn't help but add.

Jackie looked at me. After a moment, she said, "Sounds kind of like you're talking about your dad. But, obviously, you know Ruth better than I do."

"Yeah."

"Yeah."

For a few minutes we watched the garbage collectors sweep up after the parade.

"Ruth will have plenty of chances to have a good time," Jackie said quietly. "That's not going to change. Anyway, do you have anything going on? You want to hang out?"

I thought about telling her that nothing was going on, and that everything was. But then I just sighed, suddenly tired. "I don't know what I want."

Jackie grinned. "That makes two of us. No. More like four billion. Come on, let's get to the car before Gil takes off without us."

As we turned to go, a judge grabbed a megaphone and announced the parade's awards, her voice bouncing off the buildings lining Main Street. Dad's float won first place. The sophomore float didn't even qualify.

"Oh, well," Jackie said, "at least I had one last decent party at Chloe's house. Emphasis on the word *last*."

"Olivia Moore!" The judge was paging me by megaphone. My cheeks burned as I walked over to her.

"Here," she said, handing me a cheap, urn-shaped trophy. "Take this to your father. We don't want it gathering dust over at the Chamber of Commerce."

I took the thing. Jackie immediately grabbed it from me and balanced it upside down on my head.

"Queen for a day," she said, taking her hands away and leaving it there on my head. We laughed then, like real friends, and laughed even harder when the trophy toppled to the ground.

JULY 5

My fingertips are wrinkled and puckered. I must have spent a long time in the water. My hands are wrinkled and puckered, too. My arms, my legs, my whole body—wrinkled and puckered like I'm old or dead, maybe drowned.

*H*e carries her up to the bathroom when she's able, or else brings a pan of water to her bedside and sponges her clean there. He carried her up to the bathroom this afternoon, only it wasn't going so well. I stood outside the door and listened. She was panicking in the tub; it sounded like she'd grabbed him around the neck and wouldn't let go, wouldn't do anything but struggle. "Relax, Gracie," I heard him say. "Everything's okay. You can do this. Relax." She's weak as a baby, but the water still splashed. I could smell the soap he uses on her now that her skin is so sensitive, prone to rashes, dryness, and bedsores. Baby soap. Mom kept on thrashing. Dad was trying to be patient, I could tell, but he raised his voice. "Grace! You're going to hurt yourself! Or me!" And then, quiet and ashamed, "I'm sorry, Gracie. So sorry."

I was afraid he was going to come looking for me; I was afraid that he would try to escape again. "You can finish bathing her," he might say. So I climbed out my bedroom window and onto the roof. I've never done this before, though I've imagined it. The slope is steeper than I expected, the shingles hotter. But I'm going to hide here until it's quiet again, until I know she's asleep downstairs, and, best-case scenario, he's sleeping beside her. That shouldn't take too long; one of them has to give up soon.

The birds are singing in the trees like everything is grand just because it's not as hot as yesterday.

Yesterday, Jackie and I waited by the car for Gil and Charlie for close to an hour. The sun was beating down on us, and Jackie was mad as a hornet when the guys finally arrived, grinning, their arms full of bags. I might have gotten mad too, if I'd been sure that Gil and Charlie wanted me there at all.

"Calm down, Jackie," Gil said, lowering his bags

so that we could see the bottles inside. "We've been foraging for nuts and berries."

"Foraging for nuts and beer, it looks like," Jackie said, as Gil and Charlie shoved the bags into the trunk.

"Hey, there's a lot of yeast in beer." Charlie closed the trunk. "They make bread out of yeast, right? So basically we bought maybe ten loaves of bread."

Jackie clutched her stomach. "Woman does not live on bread alone."

"Chill, Jackie," Gil said affectionately.

"'Chill,' that's your mantra," Jackie muttered. "Give me the keys. I'm going to crank the air conditioner and *chill*."

"You're too young to drive." Gil got into the car and started it.

"But not too young to drink," Jackie said.

"Oh, please." Charlie jumped into the backseat. "Trojans are never too young to drink."

"I guess I'm not a Trojan, then." Jackie got in beside Gil and flipped on the air conditioner. "Come on, Livy. I need some sanity in this car."

I slipped into the backseat beside Charlie, and he immediately leaped out. I bowed my head to hide whatever my face might show. I knew it. Guys like Charlie didn't like girls like me. Guys like Charlie wouldn't want to be seen with me—wouldn't want to touch me with a ten-foot pole.

"What's this?" Charlie asked. I looked up as he grabbed the trophy from the hood of the car, where Jackie and I had left it. "Some kind of fancy hood ornament?"

"I almost forgot." I tried to sound like I didn't care. "You guys came in first. Your float, I mean."

"Awesome." Charlie sat down beside me again, slammed the door shut. "It'll make a great beer stein."

I laughed, but Jackie shook her head in disgust, saying, "Now you don't have to have those irritating little interruptions, like opening bottles or breathing. You can open all the bottles at once, dump them into the trophy, then guzzle a gallon of beer without bothering to come up for air."

"No more *bottle-us interruptus*," Gil said. "That's the scientific term."

"Ask Dr. Gil." Charlie tossed the trophy into the air; it banged against the roof.

"One dent to this car and you walk," Gil said.

I cleared my throat. "I'm supposed to take the trophy home to my dad."

"Oh. *Excuse me.*" Charlie stuffed the trophy down on the floor between his feet, then pointed out the window. "Look. It's the angel Gabriel, horn in hand."

Ed Allen was sprinting toward us, waving wildly, smiling his kind, silly smile. He kept banging his trumpet case against parked cars.

"Hey, guys?" he said, finally beside us. He leaned his head through Jackie's open window. "What's up?" He looked at me. "You really stole the show last night, Livy."

Not a question. A statement. I smiled at Ed. "You stole the show today." My cheeks burned at that. What if Charlie thought I was flirting with *Ed*?

"Thanks." Ed's brown eyes searched mine. He seemed to be waiting for me to say more, hoping I'd say more. Really listening. His freckles were nearly hidden by the high color in his cheeks, and he looked happy and confident. Nearly handsome. No, not handsome. Soulful. Like he knew what soul was.

Soulful is not necessarily fun or cool. Soulful does not necessarily make you forget.

I scooted closer to Charlie. Jackie moved over beside Gil, and Ed got in beside her. We drove through town. Music blaring, we headed west past the high school, then past my subdivision—a handful of colonials surrounded by fields of corn. We drove past the run-down trailer park—Troy City's worst eyesore, which is sinking slowly into marshy ground, or so Dad says. We turned onto the main route to the world beyond Troy City, sped by the

Dairy Queen, the truckers' Kit-Kat motel. At Jackie's insistence, we stopped at the last convenience store for miles and bought hot dogs, buns, chips, cookies. We got in the car again and drove on through farm fields that stretched to the horizon. Then we turned onto the dirt road by the abandoned drive-in theater. The hand-painted marker read Cottonwood Lane.

"Oh," I gasped.

The music was so loud that nobody heard me, nobody noticed anything different about me at all. But I was different I was sure, because I was fifteen years old again, and Mom and I were taking one of our last Saturday afternoon drives. We'd take these during the fall, when Dad was coaching football games, and the weather was too beautiful and sad to ignore. Sad because everything was dying, even though to look at it, you'd never know. This particular day the late afternoon sun was still hot enough to make us sweat, and the light was golden and thick like honey. Bees droned drunkenly among the fading, roadside flowers. Mom and I were trying to finish off the soft ice cream we'd bought at the Dairy Queen, but we were sneezing so much from the ragweed that we couldn't keep up with the drips. Our hands got stickier and stickier, until the car hit a pot-hole and Mom dipped down into her cone. A dollop of vanilla tipped her long, elegant nose. She flashed me a wry, crooked grin, brightened by the red lipstick she wore back then. Tried to lick the ice cream from her nose; failed. Rolled her dark eyes. "Oh, forget it." Tossed her soggy cone out the window. "Anyway, it's biodegradable." She whapped my elbow, knocked my cone against my chin. "Nice goatee, kiddo." We laughed.

"Let's turn here," Mom finally said, swiping away the ice cream with a flick of her hand—first my chin, then her nose. Her red fingernails glinted in the late afternoon light. "We've never been down this road." She did a U-turn, and we headed down Cottonwood Lane. "Beautiful!" she said, after we'd driven maybe a mile. "Look at those trees!"

She parked the car along the side of the road and walked briskly into an unfarmed field. She was wearing a sleeveless white shirt, and her wavy brown hair bobbed against her bare shoulders. I probably wouldn't have noticed the cottonwoods rising up out of the middle of nowhere. But there they were, giants all of them, clustered together to make a great island of shade. Their big, heart-shaped leaves stirred with a sound like soft waves.

"Come here!" Mom stopped at the base of a tree. She stretched her arms around its trunk. "I bet we can't even touch hands."

I went to the other side of the tree. Sure enough, our hands couldn't meet.

"Now you see me, now you don't." Mom peeked around the trunk, then hid behind it again. "What do you think? It would take three, maybe four people to hold hands around this thing?"

I guessed four.

Rubbing her hand against the rough bark, she stepped out from behind the cottonwood. "I bet this tree is at least a hundred years old. It's nothing like our weeping willow, not even ten and blighted." She bent down and picked up a leaf, ran her finger along its rough edge. "They're talking about putting a shopping mall out here. Bring on the plastic plants. What a waste." Mom shuddered, then stood very still, listening, it seemed, to the leaves rustling. This close I could see that the leaves had turned brittle. Their green was dulling to brown. "Come on," Mom said suddenly. "Let's see what's over that hill."

We left the trees and trudged across the field to a little hill, Mom laughing all the while that any hill would dare rise up in the middle of Illinois. She got to the top of the hill before me. "Oh, Livy," she cried out in surprise, and then she vanished, running down the other side.

Finally at the top, I saw what she'd seen: a tin-roof

shack nestled in a small, grassy valley. Mom slipped inside.

"Wait!" I called, running after her. When I reached the doorway, I stopped. I thought of wild animals and the homeless men I'd seen during a school field trip to Chicago. There wasn't a sound coming from inside the shack; Mom might as well not have been there at all. Or maybe she was lying on the floor, attacked by something I couldn't imagine. The rough wooden door hung on one hinge. I peered around it and whispered, "Mom?"

She didn't answer. I stepped over the worn rock slab that served as a front porch and edged my way into the dim room. A hailstorm had punctured the rusty roof, and streams of sunlight filtered around me to pool in small, bright circles at my feet. I waved my hand in the air but the dust only seemed to thicken. Then my eyes adjusted to the dimness, and I saw flowered wallpaper hanging in strips from mildewed walls, and on one wall an empty picture frame tilted at a crazy angle. A rocking chair, its runners broken, was shoved into one corner, and a rickety table stood nearby. On the table was a small, black sewing machine. Cautiously, I went over to it. A scrap of dusty black flannel was skewered beneath the needle. I fingered the edge of the fabric, which shredded into dry fibers. Then a spider popped from the bobbin hole and skittered across my thumb, and I bolted for the next room, which was not much more than a cracked porcelain sink, flanked with shelves covered with scat and animal tracks. There was a window above the sink, and I started to look out, but before I'd raised my hand to the torn curtains, they stirred like ghosts and sent me on to the last room.

That's where I found Mom, standing by an iron bed frame, staring at a wall. The bed frame was missing its legs; it lay flat on the floor, its rusty, sprung springs as sad and bare as a skeleton's broken bones.

"A woman lived here. I know it." Mom didn't look at me as she pointed at the wall. "Look."

Someone had painted a picture on the wall—a waterfall in a forest. The paint was chipped and peeling, but I could make out the blue cascade, white foam churning in a pool, a green tree laden with red circles like flowers or fruit.

"That's her Eden, I'd bet on it. Over here is her blue heaven." Mom pointed at another wall, another painting. It showed a blue sky dotted with white clouds, which were raining torrents of blue on a flat, empty, brown field. A rainbow arced over the clouds. "Whoever painted these pictures wanted water. Maybe she was living through a drought. Look at the last painting."

Mom led me to a third wall. On it was a painting of

a little shack, just like the one we were standing in, only the painted shack was floating on a calm lake.

"This house must miss the woman who made these paintings." Mom sighed. She seemed far away all of a sudden. Or like she'd forgotten I was there.

I cleared my throat. "How do you know it's a woman?"

"Oh, I just know." Mom smiled mysteriously. "And I read this."

She pointed to the bottom right corner of the painting. There was the name Ella, written in tiny, careful black letters.

"Ella," Mom whispered, like she was calling to the woman across the decades. Then Mom looked at her watch. Her expression tightened. "We have to go. Your father will be wanting supper."

Mom and I visited the cottonwood trees and the shack several times before the weather turned bitter. Then the next spring, she found the lump in her breast, and we never went back. I rode my bike there alone once or twice that summer, when Mom was in the hospital having her first surgery. That would have been late June. The trees were letting off their cotton; it floated like summer snow through the air, drifted into the shack, collected in great piles in the corners of the rooms. I'd lie down in these. Exhausted after my long ride, I'd doze or daydream about fairy-tale places. I'd dream that the shack was an island, and I'd been washed ashore; or the shack was a castle, and I'd been locked inside; or the shack was simply a shack, and I was newly settled, fending off wild animals and thirst, painting what I wanted on the walls.

Then the bike ride got too long, or I got too lazy, and the shack became a place I didn't want to visit. Eventually, I forgot about it altogether.

Until yesterday.

"Earth to Livy," Charlie said loudly. He waved his hand in front of my eyes; I flinched, startled. "Come in, Livy."

I looked from the fields into Charlie's eyes. He winked at me, and I tried to smile. "Roger dodger," I mumbled. "Over and out."

Charlie laughed and went back to what he had been doing: drawing an intricate maze on his cutoffs with a pen. I stared as he drew a curving line up his thigh and over his pocket. When the line turned toward his zipper, I caught my breath and looked up. Charlie was watching me, a knowing smile on his face. I crossed my arms over my chest as if that would muffle my pounding heart, and turned toward the window.

And there were the cottonwoods, standing like giants in the field, guarding the little hill. The shack would be in the valley below, floating in a sea of Queen Anne's lace, which would turn to a sea of goldenrod in August.

"Stop," I whispered.

The music was still blaring. Charlie put his hand to his ear. "What?"

"Stop!"

We kept going.

"Why stop?" Charlie said. "There's nothing here. We're almost at Goodlove. Didn't you see the sign back there?"

"No," I said dully.

I'd heard of Goodlove Forest Preserve, but I'd never been there. The place was known for tailgate parties and parking. Guys crashed cars there, girls got pregnant. Nobody went there for nature walks. Goodlove Forest Preserve was marsh, mostly. The forest part was basically a collection of cattails, with some scruffy trees down by a man-made lake. The other side of the lake was shadowed by the only steep hill for three counties—a hill that was originally garbage covered with dirt that finally grew grass. Pretty gross. You went to Goodlove to get good loving—at least, that was what Ruth had told me. I missed her, all of a sudden, sitting there in Gil's car. I wanted to be sitting beside *her* at her ailing great-uncle's picnic table, eating hamburgers, drinking Kool-Aid, while her parents kept watch.

"We have *arrived*," Gil yelled, turning the car sharply. We fishtailed down a single-lane dirt road and screeched to a stop in a dusty parking lot.

"It's just two o'clock. We've got hours until the fireworks." Jackie jumped from the car, and I got out, too. "We'll have no problem getting a spot at the top of the hill." Tugging her hair from its bun, Jackie sprinted off down a dirt path.

"We'll be down in a minute," Gil called after her. He went to the trunk, opened it, and took out two beers. He gave one to Charlie, who twisted off the cap and tipped the bottle to his lips. When he lowered the bottle, he winked at me.

"See. Aren't you glad we didn't stop? Now, come on over here, Coach Moore. No need to call plays from the sidelines." Charlie crooked his finger at me, and Gil laughed.

I tried to laugh this off. "Heel. Roll over. Fetch. Play dead," I said, backing away. And then I took off after Jackie.

I found her by the lake. She was already standing in water up to her knees.

"Come on," she said, splashing water in my direction. "It's like a bath, it's that warm."

I had just taken off my sandals when she was beside me, dragging me into the water. She jumped on my back and pushed me under. The water made my bones ache, it felt so cold after the hot air. "Yikes," I screamed, bursting above the surface.

"Spring fed!" Jackie shouted. Her hands met the top of my head and pushed me down again. Jackie was strong.

I gave up struggling and opened my eyes. This world was murky, shot through with sunlight. Sand swarmed around my feet; seaweed coiled around my legs. Jackie danced slowly beside me. I curled into a ball. Drowning might not be so bad.

Then I came up for air. Charlie stood on the shore with a beer in his hand. When he saw me, he smiled a broad, gorgeous smile that said: *There you are. I've been looking for you. You're the one I've been waiting for all day long—no, all along.*

He raised his bottle. "Cheers."

I knew then what I wanted. Not little-girl-fantasy stuff. Not Ruth. Not Dad, or even Mom, or all the things hidden beneath the surface. I wanted him.

"Cheers yourself," I said.

He said, "It's about time you got a life."

So I got blasted at Goodlove Forest Preserve. I drank and dove—off Charlie's shoulders again and again, into water that turned even murkier as the sun sank lower in the sky. We played countless games of Chicken, me perched on Charlie's shoulders—his bones and muscles moving beneath mine—Jackie on Gil's shoulders. Ed acted as referee. Our wet clothes twisted around us, plastered to our skin. Even after I was waterlogged and exhausted, I kept on playing. Charlie and I kept on winning.

Finally, Jackie said she was sick of her clothes; she was taking them off. "It'll be like I'm wearing a bikini," she said. She marched up to shore, undressed to her bra and panties, and draped her wet things over a bush to dry. Snapping her underwear securely into place, she marched back into the lake and sank down. "See," she said. "I'm covered up to my neck. Totally modest." The guys didn't bother to get out of the water; they just stripped down to their boxer shorts and heaved their sopping clothes up onto the sand. Then they looked at me.

Charlie swept his long hair from his eyes. "We're waiting."

My head was spinning from the beer. I giggled. *Giggled!* Charlie swam toward me, his hands pressed palm to palm, cutting through the water like a shark's fin. I took off for shore. I scampered across the hot sand and stood in the shade of a weeping willow tree. Slowly, I shed my shirt and shorts, and dropped them in the sand. It was easier than I thought it would be, because the branches nearly concealed me. I could pretend that I was alone; I was simply getting more comfortable.

I adjusted my dingy white bra, my fraying pink underpants. My underwear looked dirty even when it wasn't. I needed Mom to take me shopping.

Suddenly, I couldn't go back to the lake, to them. Teeth chattering, I froze beneath the tree. Think, I thought. Get a grip.

And I thought of Dad standing on the sidelines, how he always kept a grip on the game, how he hardened his expression to command respect. I hardened my expression. Then I made myself *stop* thinking of Dad. I parted the willow branches. Not meeting anyone's eyes, I walked into the water. I hid as much of me as I could beneath the surface.

"All right!" Charlie applauded. "Join the club."

I let out a shaky whoop of joy. No one seemed to think I was stupid. Charlie paddled toward me, grinning. He passed me his beer. I took a swig, and that stopped my trembling.

The afternoon passed that way, Charlie passing me

beers, me drinking them. We were swimming lazily now, talking about everyday stuff, like movies and television shows.

"When it comes to music, I keep going backward, not forward," Jackie said. "Oldies, but goodies. You know. The Stones. *Exile on Main Street.* I'm so into that CD."

"Um, *record*, Jackie. If you're so into it, you should be listening to the original vinyl."

This was Gil. Jackie ignored him.

"And Billie Holiday. The way she sings 'Strange Fruit,' for instance. And Edith Piaf. I don't know French, but I know exactly what she means."

"I know what you mean," Ed said.

We shifted in the water; we looked at Ed. I think we'd nearly forgotten he was there. His freckled shoulders stiffened. The choppy water licked his collarbones like it wanted him to relax again. I thought of his trumpet playing—how he fingered those valves, poured his breath through that golden bell. Not stiff at all.

"Who do you like?" I asked.

Ed smiled. "Louis Armstrong, of course." He gazed up at the sky. "And Chet Baker. Miles Davis. Dizzy Gillespie." He began to recite the names of other musicians—musicians I'd never heard of—his voice deepening and softening to a chant. Still chanting, he sank down under the water. He forced air to the surface, blowing bubbles like a song from the deep, and we laughed.

"Miles is *it*," Jackie said, when Ed came up again, sputtering.

"How about old books? Do you like *Gone with the Wind*? I'm reading that right now."

This was me, offering something about myself that they couldn't have known or assumed. An actual fact.

"'Frankly, my dear, I don't give a damn,'" Charlie drawled.

Something I only should have shared with Mom.

"Shut up, Charlie." Jackie rolled her eyes. "But, yeah. With that book, it's kind of like, been there, done that. In seventh grade."

"Seventh grade. Yeah. Me, too," I said quickly. This was a lie. "But I like rereading things sometimes." This wasn't a lie. "To see where I am now, compared to where I was then."

I shut my trap. Where am I now? I wondered. Where have I been?

But Jackie nodded like she knew exactly what I meant.

And then Charlie spent a long time diving down and grabbing Jackie and me around the legs when we least expected it. We fought to keep our footing, but he always pulled us under.

It was Ed who pointed his beer bottle at the horizon and said, "The sun is going down."

"A fire," Gil said. "That's what we need."

He charged up onto the shore, pulled on his jeans, and started collecting wood. Ed joined him, his skinny body sunburned pink. Together they built a pyramid of branches. Gil went to the car and returned with some matches and a newspaper. When a small, fierce fire was crackling, Jackie and Charlie got out of the water. While they were busy dressing, I got out too, grabbed my clothes, and hid beneath the willow tree again. My pale arms and legs looked as willowy as the tree limbs, though maybe not quite so graceful. I have Mom's body, I thought. I squatted down at this, like something had punched me in the stomach. Even when she is gone, I will have her body. For the rest of my life, I'll look at me and see her.

When Mom came home after her first mastectomy, she needed my help like never before. She was always asking me to do this or that, and she seemed angry at me half the time—like I never did this or that quickly enough or in the right way. It seemed like it was my fault that everything was so hard for her, and I kept trying to figure out how to act older than fifteen, maybe more like forty-one, Mom's age. I was too scared by the changes in her to get mad about all the weird responsibility. Too scared of the changes that might come. Too scared, all the time. One day, Mom screamed, "Help!" so loudly that she sounded like she was in danger. I ran upstairs and found her standing by her unmade bed, holding a blanket in her hands like she had forgotten what a blanket was for. She looked at me and said, "Help." I took hold of one end of the blanket, and as we tucked it in, the rounded neck of her nightgown fell open, and I saw the scar on her chest where her breast had been—a jagged slash the color of dried blood. She saw me looking. She turned her back on me and sank down on the bed. Then she said, "I don't need your help after all." I ran from the room. I went to the kitchen and washed my hands with hand soap, then with dish soap; but it felt like my hands still weren't clean, like something contagious had touched my skin.

Kneeling beneath the willow tree, I remembered that day. My hands moved to my breasts. Carefully, I cupped them through my wet bra. They're not much bigger than plums, with nipples as soft as cotton balls. I've read a few romance novels—enough to know that hard nipples are supposed to be sexy. I pinched my nipples but they didn't change. If I had been kneeling in front of a mirror, they would have looked back at me like two pale, bland eyes. I pinched harder; I pushed, wincing. My breasts hurt all the time. I've never told anyone this. They hurt more, the harder I pushed. I began to probe. It was like I was looking for something, there beneath the willow, and I found it. Something right at the core, hard and small and unmoving.

Please God, let it be my ribs.

"Surprise." Charlie stepped through the willow branches.

I crossed my arms over my chest. I couldn't breathe.

Charlie laughed. He clapped his hands over his eyes. "Whoops."

Trembling, I snatched up my clothes and hunched over them. Sand drizzled from the folds and stuck to my damp skin.

"Can I look now?"

I nodded.

"Is that a 'yes'?"

"Yes," I managed to whisper.

Charlie knelt down near me in the sand. "You've been, like, in hiding forever. Are you spending the night here, or what?"

I tried to smile. "Maybe."

"Then maybe I will, too."

The muscles in my arms and legs tightened; I was ready to bolt. But Charlie tucked a wet strand of hair behind my ear. Something about the way he did that helped me relax. He picked up a stick and began to trace a pattern in the sand—X's and O's, wild lines and arrows. I loosened my grip on my clothes, sat back on my heels. My clothes tumbled from my lap to the ground, and I didn't do anything to cover myself.

"Looks like a game plan," I said.

"I guess it is." Charlie shrugged. "I can't get away from football, I guess. It's my ticket out of here. Your old man is, really."

Dad, I thought, and looked quickly around. But it was only willow branches, swaying and sighing in the breeze.

"What do you mean, 'my old man'?" I asked.

"Oh, you know. College. Scouts. Letters of recommendation. Your old man wrote some great letters for Gil—said Gil did well for himself, 'in spite of all obstacles.' That's what your dad wrote: 'In spite of all obstacles, Gil Perez is a fine young man.' Financial obstacles, I guess he meant. Me and Gil are alike in that way. We're tired of living on the wrong side of the tracks. We want to live on the right side. Some day."

"Oh."

"*Oh?* You don't get it, do you?"

"I'm trying." I grabbed my clothes again. "To get it."

Charlie watched as I began to fumble with my shirt. After a moment he said, "You know that trailer park we passed on the way out here?"

I nodded. "I drive past it all the time."

"Right. You drive *past* it. You and everyone else who can. You and the whole world that matters." A willow branch lay at Charlie's feet; he picked it up and began to strip off the leaves. "Well, that dump is where I live."

"Oh." I was cold all of a sudden. And I couldn't seem to get my stupid shirt on.

"Not everybody has a coach for a dad." Charlie stood. He whipped the willow branch; it whistled through the air. "By the way, Jackie and Gil live in the park, too. Only, I wouldn't let on you know. They're not too crazy about the place either, what with the way their mom has to work two jobs to keep them there. If you're going to work two jobs, at least you could live in a condo, or something. Now, come on." Charlie snapped his finger like I was a dog, then held out his hand. I took it, and he hoisted me to my feet. "You need help getting dressed?"

I shook my head.

"I didn't think so. But what the hell, right?"

He grabbed my clothes and had my arms through the sleeves of my shirt before I could protest. Briskly, he buttoned my shirt to the top button. It was tight around my throat. I fingered my collar and Charlie laughed.

"Step in," he said, snapping the wrinkles from my shorts. I stepped in. Then Charlie's hands moved for my zipper.

"I can do that," I said. Charlie grinned, but he drew back his hands. I zipped my shorts. We stood looking at each other. I could feel his breath on my face. My skin was tingling; the damp clothes made me feel even colder. Certain things had come sharply into focus: the grains of sand dusting Charlie's forehead and cheeks, the golden strands of his hair.

"I can see your pulse." He pressed his fingertips to my neck. I could feel my blood surging; I could hear it.

"Livy? Charlie, what are you doing to her?" Jackie's voice made us both jump.

"Be right there," Charlie called in a high-pitched, little boy's voice. *"Mom."* Roughly, he rubbed his hand across my neck, then he turned to part the branches. "Come on, I'm starving anyway," he said.

I took a deep breath, adjusted my clothes, then followed him into the open. Jackie was setting out food, and

Charlie was already beside her, grabbing chips from a bag. He didn't look at me when I walked up, but she did, closely. She was the only one of us who hadn't been drinking, and her gaze was too steady for me. I looked away to see Ed drop a hot dog on the sand, then spear it at a crazy angle on a stick and lower it right into the flames. Gil laughed as the hot dog ignited. Jackie helped Ed blow out the flames.

Now I am walking past Charlie and not looking at him, I thought. Now I am bending over and pulling a hot dog from the packet. It's slippery, hold on tight. Now I am finding a stick and picking it up. I'm cleaning the stick on my shorts.

It went on like that, until I actually sat down and wolfed two hot dogs, several handfuls of chips, five cookies. I felt a little better then. The sun was a red sliver on the horizon, and I could look Jackie right in the eyes.

She said, "We'd better head up the hill."

Gil, Charlie, and Ed grunted in agreement, but nobody moved.

Jackie stood. "Ready, Livy?"

I stole a glance at Charlie, but he was staring blankly at the lake, blowing into a beer bottle. The sound he made was low and mournful. I got to my feet, and the earth swayed.

"Steady, there." Jackie linked her arm through mine.

We walked around the lake to the hill. Jackie practically had to pull me up it, and I groaned the whole way. Once at the top, though, I could see why she wanted to come. The lights of Troy City glittered in the distance like jewels scattered from a broken necklace. We lay flat on our backs in the patchy grass and watched the sky darken from blue to purple to black. Then the fireworks started.

"Are you up there watching?" Jackie called to someone behind the shimmering sky.

Ed's trumpet sounded, and I realized that he, Charlie, Gil, and lots of other people had gathered close by. Everyone sang along as Ed belted out the "Star Spangled Banner." You're better than Louis, I wanted to say. Or you will be someday. After the first verse, Charlie lay down beside me. He was on my right and Jackie was on my left. I stopped singing. I held very still. This is a dream, I thought. If I move, I'll wake up. But then Charlie's arm was against mine, and he took my hand, and the sky wasn't the only thing that felt electric and ablaze. I'm happy, I thought. Happy. I could almost taste the word like sugar on my tongue.

During the finale, Charlie rolled over and kissed me. My heart boomed like the fireworks. I didn't care if he heard, because I could feel his heart pounding, too, against my body. Then Charlie's hand brushed against my breasts. I sat bolt upright, suddenly terrified. I wanted to run, but instead I tried to focus on the clear notes bursting from Ed's trumpet. Even under my clothes, my breasts burned like fire had touched there, or ice. Charlie sat up, too. Out of the corner of my eye, I could see him staring dully at the sky, like nothing special was happening there at all. That's it, I thought. I've ruined everything. I had to bite my tongue to keep from crying.

On the way home, Charlie sat in the front seat with Gil, who, for once, didn't turn on the radio. Gil loves fireworks, it turns out, better than almost anything. He wanted to remember each one. We listened to him go on. Charlie, Jackie, and Ed joined in once in a while. I might as well have been a shadow.

JULY 6

Dad is teaching phys ed. I'm sitting at the back of the class. Charlie is sitting near the front, with Jackie, Gil, Ruth, Ed, and Chloe. They are with the cool kids. They *are* the cool kids.

This must be a health and hygiene unit, because a Visible Woman doll is on Dad's desk. She is bigger than Barbie, and she stands solidly on flat feet, not those precarious Barbie toes. But like Barbie, Visible Woman has hard, perfect curves—torpedo-like breasts and rounded hips that narrow to a smooth, rigid waist. Visible Woman seems indestructible, like nothing could penetrate her clear, plastic skin.

Of course, I know about the thin slit that runs Visible Woman's length. I know how to open her like a book. I've untangled her guts and taken them out, held their dull, ugly colors in my hands. But in the dream, it's Dad's job to show her to me.

Dad's nervous, sitting by the doll on the desk. He sticks his hands in his pockets, rattles keys and coins. He says, "Who here knows anything about the facts of life?"

Silence. I stare at the back of Charlie's head. His hair shines like a halo. I will him to turn

106

around and smile at me, but he slumps in his seat. The next thing I know, my hand is in the air.

Dad says, "Name, please?"

Charlie still doesn't turn around, not even as he says, "Olive Oyl."

I cannot stop myself. I lift my hands to my shirt. I start undoing buttons, one by one. Amazed and horrified, Dad opens his mouth. Dad is going to say something to make me stop.

I woke up before Dad got the chance. My nightgown was twisted around me. I got out of bed to straighten it, and then I walked to the window and lifted the screen. The sun wasn't up yet; even the birds were still asleep. But I was wide awake and hot, and I wanted out. I climbed onto the roof. I scooted down to the gutter, looked over the edge. There was maybe fifteen feet between me and the ground. I jumped.

The next thing I knew I was lying in the long, wet

grass, unable to breathe. My bones ached. I gasped and coughed and finally found my breath, then tested my arms and legs, my neck. Cautiously, I sat up. I was okay. I might be one big bruise, especially around my hip, but I'd finally done it, the thing I used to imagine doing when I was little and so afraid of fire: I'd jumped from the roof. I could do it better next time. Or I could do it worse, if I wanted. I smiled at this thought. I felt powerful. If I were ten years younger, I probably would have tried this with a cape. Still smiling, I stood and came face-to-face with Mom.

She was leaning against the living room window, watching me. I couldn't tell if she recognized me. Maybe she thought I was an animal, an angel, or an alien, or maybe she thought I was a dream. But she was up. Standing. I stretched out my hand and tapped on the glass. Hello, I was trying to say. It's all right, I'm not hurt, I won't hurt you. Please, don't get Dad. I could make out his dark shape lying on the hospital bed behind her.

Mom turned away from the window. She headed toward the bed, listing like a sailboat in a gale. I looked down at the imprint of my body in the grass. Even when I fall from the sky, I thought, she is too sick to care.

When I looked up again, Mom was gone. She had left

the living room. For the first time in weeks, she had left the living room—left her bed—without Dad's help. She is wandering the house, I thought. She might try the stairs and fall down them. She might try the roof.

I hobbled as quickly as I could to the back door. When I opened it, Mom stepped out. She drifted past me and started across the lawn. "Let me help you," I said. But she pushed my arm away. She went to the willow tree, ducked under the branches, sank to the ground. She leaned against the trunk. I knelt beside her.

"What are you doing out here without a robe?" she said.

I laughed, suddenly giddy, then pressed my hand to my aching hip. "What are you doing out here at all?"

"What are *you*—" Mom gave me a little smile. "Never mind. Ask me something. There must be something you need to know."

I tried to sound carefree. "What's your favorite color?"

"Red." She rubbed her forehead against the trunk. "Ask me. You can ask me."

I made myself laugh, even though it hurt and nothing was funny. My hand slipped from my hip to my ribs to my breasts. I asked, "Will I get cancer, too?"

Mom caught her breath. "No," she said loudly,

almost shouting. She rubbed her head against the trunk, but too hard, scraping her skin.

"What the fuck," Dad said, "are you doing?"

He was hunkered down beside us. "What the fuck?" he said again. Dad doesn't swear, not even when his team is losing bad. He pointed his finger at me, jabbed his finger three times in the air: "What. The. Fuck."

"Quiet, Ward. Please. The neighbors." Mom touched her forehead. She studied the faint smear of blood on her fingers. She said, "The two of you are going to church."

Dad and I both turned to look at her. From the corner of my eye, I could see that his mouth was open in horror and amazement, just like in my dream. My mouth was open, too. I closed it.

"Red," Mom said dreamily. "I can still bleed." And then she glared at Dad. "Stop it," she said to his openmouthed horror, to his amazement. "Just stop it. You are taking our daughter to church. Today. You are taking her."

Dad tried to persuade Mom to go back into the house, but she started to cry. So the three of us stayed under the willow tree for some time while she calmed down. Dad wouldn't look at me, Mom wouldn't look away from me, and I didn't know where to look. I closed my eyes and listened to the birds wake up. Finally, Mom fell asleep in Dad's arms, and he carried her off to bed.

Then he and I did Sunday morning stuff—put on decent clothes (me a summer dress, him a suit), ate a decent breakfast to get us through the long service. When Mrs. Ford was standing over Mom, trying to wash dirt from her scrape while she slept, we got into the Bonneville and drove off. I stared out the window at the cornfields flashing past. In the quiet, I could hear Dad swallow. He kept swallowing, gulping as if his throat were tight. A couple of times, he started to say something, then didn't.

"When we get home," he finally said as we pulled into the church parking lot, "you're grounded."

"What? Why?" I stared at Dad. For the first time in my life, being grounded mattered.

"Because I said so." He yanked the keys from the ignition. "Someone's got to take some responsibility here."

"Mom said you were supposed to take me to church, not take some responsibility."

"Same difference."

I slammed my fist hard against the door. "I thought I was supposed to take care of myself. You said that too." I hit the door again.

"Watch it. One week grounded just turned into two."

I laughed softly. Under my breath I said, "Oh, you're so responsible."

Dad heard. He hit his door harder than I could ever hit anything. The car rocked.

"I am responsible for everything. Everything! And look what happens when I let up. You take off to places without telling me. You think I don't know? I know. And then you pull some stunt like this morning. If you hadn't been outside, your mother wouldn't have been outside." Dad opened the door and got out of the car. "Do you know what that kind of exertion could do to her?"

"But I didn't make her come outside. She wanted—"

He slammed the door. He looked at me through the window in a way that made me go quiet, and then he stomped off toward the church. Dumb as a sheep, I got out and followed him. From the sidewalk, I watched as he marched up the steps.

The last time the three of us attended a service, Mom left in the middle of Pastor Bob's sermon. He was preaching about the body's corruption. "We must die to this life, and live for the next," he kept saying. "This flesh is only a rusty cage for the soul." Maybe Dad was remembering this too, because he paused at the heavy oak door and bowed his head. But then Sheriff Byrne was at his side. He slung his arm around Dad's shoulder and guided him into the sanctuary.

I started to follow, but someone called my name. I

turned around, and there was Ruth, in cutoffs and a green-and-yellow Trojans T-shirt, cradling a black backpack in her arms.

"They need help in the nursery," she said.

I shrugged.

"Go tell your dad that you'll be helping out in the nursery today. Then meet me back here. Go on." She winked at me.

I found Dad sitting by Sheriff Byrne in our old family pew, the third one from the front. When I told him about the nursery, he started to shake his head, but then Sheriff Byrne said, "Now, there's a good citizen," and Dad waved me off. I went back outside. It took me a moment to spot Ruth standing at the end of the block in front of the A&W. She was holding two large cups in her hands. I ran to her, and she handed me a root beer float. I took a sip, and it tasted great—smoother and richer than anything I'd tasted for weeks. Ruth grinned and pointed at my mouth. I licked foam from my upper lip.

"I'm grounded," I said.

"Me too."

"No way."

"Yes way." Ruth raised her float in a toast, and we knocked cups. "I went to Uncle Will's shindig, but then I ditched it. My cousin-once-removed gave me a ride to a party at the VFW hall. Everyone there was way past high school." Ruth patted her backpack. "I brought some party favors."

We walked across the street to the park. There's a wooden bridge there that spans the one pond in town. The pond is man-made, and it always smells like dead fish and mildew. But ducks and geese bob on its surface, and the surrounding trees make it a shady, quiet place. When Ruth and I were in junior high, we used to sit on the bridge a lot. We used to go there and talk about everything.

Now we sat on the bridge and downed our floats without saying a word. It was enough to be there together, like old times. When Ruth was finished, she set her cup down and wrapped her arms around her stomach.

"Oooh," she moaned. "Freezer burn. It's like a dagger. I drank that way too fast—or maybe just in time." She nodded toward the street, where the green sedan was slowing to a stop. She stood and waved.

"Gil's here?" I tried to sound easygoing, but where there was Gil, there was Charlie. "I thought this was just you and me."

"It was. Hey, Jackie!" she shouted. Jackie had emerged from the car. She tossed some trash into a garbage can, then gave an elegant wave and slipped back into the passenger seat. Ruth grinned at me. "Come on, we can be delinquents together. What have we got to lose? We're already grounded." She narrowed her eyes. "Or maybe you'd rather go help out in the nursery?"

I shook my head.

"Well come on, then." Ruth took off toward the car.

Charlie leaned out the car window and flashed his fingers in a sign of victory or peace. Whatever—he was signaling me, I realized. There was no reason for him to catch Ruth's attention; she was already on her way. I took a deep breath. Then I ran after Ruth, toward Charlie.

I was barely in the backseat, squeezed between Charlie and Ed, when Gil floored the accelerator and we sped away from the curb. We tore down Main Street, which was as empty as could be on a Sunday morning, and careened around a corner.

"I'm out of here!" Gil shouted. "I'm out of this two-bit town. Michigan State, here I come! I'm going to blow you away!"

"Go M.S.U.!" Ruth cheered. She was squeezed between Jackie and the passenger door.

"I've heard they have a great team," I said, trying to make conversation like we weren't on the brink of an accident.

No one was listening to me. Everyone but Jackie was

laughing too hard. "Watch it!" she shrieked as we sped toward a red light.

Gil slammed on his brakes, and we screeched to a stop, the smell of hot rubber heavy in the air. We sat in silence for a moment, listening to the engine idle.

"You're a lousy driver, you know it, Gil?" Jackie climbed over Ruth, opened the door, and got out of the car. "Especially when you're in this kind of mood. Go ahead and get your ya yas out without me. I'll walk home."

The light turned green; the car behind us honked. Jackie slammed the door and stepped to the curb.

"I've never even had a ticket," Gil yelled.

"You're holding up traffic." Charlie pounded his fists on Gil's headrest. I found myself leaning away from him, against Ed. Ed smiled at me, and I couldn't help but smile, too; his smile is that sweet. But then I quickly moved back to the center of the seat. Charlie kept pounding, until finally Gil sped away, leaving Jackie standing at the street corner. He turned a corner, then slowed to the speed limit. I let out a sigh of relief, and Ruth looked back at me and laughed. Then she scooted closer to Gil.

"Jackie's right," she said. "You're antsy. You need to find a way to let off some steam."

"You're ready to move on, like you said, right, Gil?" Ed said. "You're ready to play a little college ball?"

"You got that right." Gil stopped at an intersection. He draped his arms over the steering wheel and flexed his fingers. "This town feels so small. You know what I mean?"

Yes. We knew. It did. Definitely, we agreed. Then Ed suggested we go to the A & W, and Ruth groaned.

"Boring," she said. She slipped her arm around Gil's shoulder. "There's something I want to do and I need your help. Believe me, you'll get your ya yas out."

"The more ya yas, the better," Gil said.

"Uh-oh. He's stalkin'." Charlie gave a howl. "Say 'baa,' Ruthie. The big bad wolf has got a taste for fresh lamb."

Ruth ignored Charlie. She brushed tendrils of hair from her forehead. "I'll spell it out for you in two words: fire works."

"Fireworks." My heart began to race. "That's one word, I think."

Charlie laughed.

"Fireworks?" Gil flicked his eyebrows at Ruth.

She pulled her backpack from the floor of the car, unzipped it, held it open for Gil to see. He looked inside and gave a low whistle.

"Heavy artillery," he said.

Charlie leaned over the front seat and looked inside

Ruth's backpack. Then he looked up at her, his eyes wide. "Wow. You have my respect."

Ed looked as well, then immediately sat back. His face was white; even his lips had gone pale. "Do you know how to ignite those things? M-80s and all?"

Now I had to see. Ruth's backpack was stuffed with fireworks: bottle rockets, cherry bombs, and other brightly colored and black devices that I didn't recognize. I stared at her stash, my skin prickling. "Where did you get all that?" I asked.

"I told you." Ruth smiled smugly. "Last night while you guys were communing with nature, I was doing some serious partying."

"Aren't those things illegal?" I said. "I mean, don't people have to go to Missouri or some place to buy them?"

Ruth zipped her backpack and nonchalantly tossed it back onto the car floor. I flinched and Ed let out a yelp.

"The guy didn't give me his name," Ruth said. "But I don't think it was Missouri."

Gil and Charlie thought that was really funny.

"Safely, I mean?" Ed said, as if he'd never stopped talking. "Do you know how to ignite those things safely? M-80s and all?"

"I figured Gil would know." Ruth lightly rested her hand on Gil's shoulder. "Since you really like fireworks."

"Oh, brother," Charlie muttered.

Gil rubbed his jaw. "I've set off a few fireworks in my time."

"I assume you don't mean that metaphorically?" Ed said.

Charlie let out another howl. "Nice going, Ed. That was funny."

We all laughed at that—the kind of laughter that Ruth and I used to call church-laughter, the edgy laughter that comes when you're not supposed to laugh at all. Then suddenly we stopped laughing.

"So," Ruth said. "Are you up for it?"

"I am," Charlie said.

"You bet." Gil cracked his knuckles. "I've got the touch. Right, Ed?"

Ed didn't answer. He plucked at his lower lip—at a callus there that I'd never noticed before, that must have come from trumpet-playing. The callus reddened beneath Ed's fingers; it looked tender, like he'd just been stung by a bee.

A car pulled up behind us at the intersection and honked. Everyone jumped—Gil most of all. Suddenly serious, he started driving. We turned down one street, then another. I finally asked where we were going.

Gil cleared his throat. "What do you have in mind,

Ruth?" He spoke politely, like this was a formal occasion.

"Church," she said quickly—an answer she'd prepared. "Not inside church, of course. But outside—right outside. Everyone is going to think it's the Second Coming."

I caught my breath. Dad.

"Ruth?" I said quietly. "Getting grounded isn't that big a deal, is it?"

"Maybe we should go, like, way out in the country?" Ed said.

Ruth ignored Ed. "It's not about getting grounded. Not really." She took a quick look at her watch, then threw her arms around Gil and gave him a quick, fierce hug. "Let's go. Drive!"

Gil drove toward the church, carefully minding the speed limit. Ed kept giving me tense smiles, but Charlie didn't even look at me. He was drumming his fingers on his knees, mouthing the words to some song I didn't recognize.

We parked behind an abandoned gas station that was right beside the church. Ruth got out of the car and quickly unloaded her backpack. When she was finished, ten fireworks lay in a neat row before her. She reached in the backpack again, pulled out a book of matches, tossed it at Gil. He caught it.

"You kept matches with fireworks?" Ed said. "That's crazy."

"Silly me." Ruth wrinkled her nose.

Ed's gaze darted from Gil to Ruth and back again. "Be careful, okay? Don't get too crazy?"

"*You're* making us crazy!" Charlie gave Ed a shove. "Quit being such a freak."

Ed frowned. He kicked a crumpled soda can into the gutter. "I'm not a freak."

"We know, Ed," Ruth said.

"You're an artist," I said.

Ed glanced at me, smiling and grateful, but then Charlie and Gil laughed, and, as quickly, Ed's eyes filled with tears. He stared at the ground, and I thought of Mom, crying that morning before dawn, and then of Dad, sitting in the sanctuary in the same old spot. In that moment, I hated Ruth. I hated Ruth, Gil, and Charlie. I hated me.

"This is stupid," I said.

Ruth glared at me. She grabbed a bright green rocket and gave it to Gil. In his hands it looked like a toy.

Gil turned to Charlie. "Want to ride shotgun?"

Charlie narrowed his eyes. "What's that supposed to mean?"

"You know—be my right-hand man. Pass me what I tell you to, just like in football."

"Sure, Coach," Charlie muttered.

"From left to right, that's how we'll shoot them off," Gil said, striking a match.

There was the faint smell of sulfur, and then the flame like a forked tongue, flicking and darting in the soft breeze. Gil lit the rocket, and a spark sizzled. The wick writhed, snakelike.

"Throw the thing!" Ed yelled, and Gil did. The rocket sailed up into the air, a red arrow aimed at a blue sky, piercing a white cloud—almost.

But not quite. The rocket exploded with a terrible bang when it was not much higher than the telephone wires. The sound was so loud that the gas station windows rattled. I covered my face with my hands, afraid the windows would break. But when I lowered my hands, the glass was intact—plastered with No Trespassing signs, but intact.

Now Charlie worked fast, and Gil worked faster. Together, they set off one firework, then another— *bam, bam.* I clapped my hands over my ears. Blue smoke curled in the air, sparks flew, the ground trembled. Ed stood beside me, his hands also shielding his ears. Ruth grinned at the sky like nothing in the world could bother her—let alone a little noise.

Charlie grabbed a red stick with a short fuse. He passed it to Gil.

Ed grabbed my arm. "That's an M-80. That's, like, a half a stick of dynamite."

My knees went weak; I sank down into a squat, pulling Ed with me.

Efficiently, effortlessly, Gil struck another match and held it to the wick. Then he tossed the M-80 into the air.

When it went off, everyone else dropped to the ground. Shards of glass rained down behind us. The sound seemed to go on for a long time. Slowly, I looked up. Slowly, I stood. I wasn't bleeding; neither were Ed, Gil, Charlie, or Ruth. There were holes where the gas station windows had been, but we were all intact. Gil pointed to the car, and we ran toward it. We got inside just as a crowd of men surged down the church steps. Sheriff Byrne was leading them, followed by Pastor Bob and Dad, who cupped his hands to his mouth and shouted, "Livy? Where are you? Are you okay? Livy?" His words came to me faintly, through the ringing in my ears. But I could make out the urgency in his voice. When I was a little girl, Dad sometimes called for me like that. Mom did more often. I opened the car door and started to get out.

"Are you nuts?" Ruth lunged over the seat and pulled me back. She slammed the door and turned to Gil. "Hit it!"

Gil shifted into reverse, and we flew backward out of the alley.

"Faster!" Charlie shouted.

We screeched out of the alley into the street, then raced through town. We sped for miles into the country, down Cottonwood Lane, past the giant trees and the shack, and into Goodlove Forest Preserve. Gil parked the car, and for what seemed like a long time, we sat frozen, silent, except for the sound of our breathing. Then Ruth put her head in her hands and started to laugh. One by one, Charlie, Gil, Ed, and I joined in.

Gil pulled an amber flask of something fierce from the glove compartment, and soon enough we were laughing harder, most of the bottle drained. Then we were running toward the lake, stripping off our clothes as we went, tossing them in the air, laughing as they fell. Ed flapped his thin, sunburned arms like wings and circled around me, whistling like a robin—exactly like a robin. My shirt landed on Charlie's head. I laughed as he swept it to the ground, buried it beneath the sand, then spun around and grabbed my hand. We were all down to our underwear now. Charlie and I ran together into the shockingly cold water, went down together, swam, then surfaced again, gasping and laughing and ready for whatever was next.

Then Ruth was in Gil's arms and they were drifting off, heading deeper and deeper into darker water. They kissed, tongues flicking, and as I watched, Ruth's bra came free. For a moment it bobbed like a water lily on the small waves; in the next moment it sank. Gil and Ruth sank down too; they stayed underwater for what seemed forever. When they burst up for air, I heard Ruth's strange, new laughter, saw the hard radiance on her face, and I knew something deep inside her had changed.

I turned, and Charlie was right in front of me. He moved in close, until his face blurred into the face of someone I didn't recognize, and his mouth was on mine. I started shaking, with cold and something else. I clenched my teeth to stop their chattering, and Charlie groaned, put his hand to my jaw and pried my mouth open, forced his tongue inside. My teeth came down on his tongue with the chattering I couldn't control, but he seemed to think I'd intended it—the groan he gave this time was all pleasure and nothing else. His hands went down under the water, grabbed my legs, and wrapped them around his hips. Then he was carrying me through the water. We danced together that way, kissing and touching like we'd been born to do it, and suddenly I wasn't cold at all.

Who knows what might have happened if Ed hadn't exploded the last M-80.

JULY 7

The house is on fire. I jump from my bed to a rug, from that to another rug, and then to another. Through the rugs, the hot floor burns my feet. The door is a wall of flames. A doll's head melts; a dog-eared copy of *Gone with the Wind* turns to cinders and whirls away, a black butterfly. Dresser, nightstand, and lamp burst like bombs, like M-80s, loud enough to wake the dead.

*W*hen I crash, and I do crash, not at night so much anymore, but at crazy times—like early in the afternoon—I sleep so deeply I might as well be dead. Or it feels that way. Until I wake up like right now, later in the afternoon, and realize that even that far gone, I wasn't safe from dreams. My bed might be whole, and my dresser, nightstand, and lamp, too. But this girly-purple room might as well be painted in blood. I'm heading for my open window, for the pitched roof and steely sky, but I still can't get away from the perilous scene by the lake.

When Ed set off the M-80, the lake seemed to shiver and quake like jelly in a bowl. Small waves chopped against Charlie's shoulders and my hands resting there. The waves sounded like kisses. Then Ed screamed, drowning out this sound and every other. I turned away from Charlie to see Gil and Ruth emerge half dressed from beneath the willow—*my* willow, I thought, Charlie's and mine. Struggling into their clothes, they tore across the beach to where Ed knelt, his hands raised in the air. He screamed and screamed; he screamed in Gil's face. Gil put his hand on Ed's shoulder. Ed jerked away and fell to the sand.

Charlie pushed my legs from his waist and charged toward shore. I followed him through water that felt as thick and heavy as mud. Finally, I stood with the others beside Ed. I took one look at his hands, and I closed my eyes.

"He's out cold," Charlie said.

"He's burned himself bad," Gil said.

Charred flesh. I smelled it.

Ruth said, "Somebody get his hands out of the sand."

I opened my eyes. Lift it, I thought, like Ed was something I had to dissect in science lab. I lifted one arm;

Charlie lifted the other. Sand coated oozing flesh. I looked away, gritting my teeth.

"I'll get the car," Gil said. "I'll drive it right up to him. That way—"

"That way we'll get stuck. We'll never get out of here." Charlie glared at Gil. "Great idea."

"Got a better one?" Gil said.

"Charlie's right—" Ruth began.

"Shut up." Gil turned on her. "We're in trouble. Big trouble."

Ruth twisted her hands in her hair. "Ed's the one who—"

"Don't you get it?" Gil said savagely. "If you hadn't brought the fireworks, this never would have happened. This is your fault."

If you hadn't been outside, your mother wouldn't have been outside. I shook Dad's voice from my head. Ruth was crying now.

"We have to carry him."

Charlie, Gil, and Ruth looked at me, and I realized that I was the one talking. I said, "We have to carry him to your car, Gil. It's the only way."

"Take his arm," Charlie told Ruth. Ruth's face contorted, but she carefully lifted Ed's arm from Charlie's hands. Charlie grabbed Ed's ankles, and Gil gripped Ed under his armpits. I held Ed's other arm steady. We lifted him up. He was so thin, and so heavy. Ruth and I worked to keep his hands clear of the sharp-edged beach grass. Stumbling, staggering, we somehow got him to the car.

We laid him in the backseat, then scrambled for the rest of our clothes. It took me the longest, finding my shirt in the sand, and everyone swore at me when I finally ran back to the car. "Fuck you," I replied. I eased myself in beside Ed, lifted his head and rested it in my lap. He had gone so pale, his thin face looked almost translucent, his freckles floating just beneath the surface of his skin like flecks of rust. Wet sand caked his bare feet. His pulpy hands lay on his belly, twitching. Ruth lifted his legs, slipped into the seat, and lowered his feet into her lap. Charlie and Gil rode in the front.

We were mostly quiet as we drove. The little bit we talked, we tried to imagine what had happened, one of us starting a sentence, another finishing it. Maybe Ed felt left out when we were in the water and that's why he went back to the beach. Maybe he started looking for his clothes on the trail we had scattered behind us during our sprint to the lake. Maybe if his trumpet had been there, too, he would have found it and played, and what happened wouldn't have happened. But instead, Ed found the M-80 that Charlie dropped in the sand by his shorts. He found matches in the pocket of Gil's shirt. Maybe he looked out at the lake and saw us there, occupied; then maybe he felt sad or lonely or angry—this is me thinking, now, not the others. And then maybe Ed decided to try to be like Gil, the way Ed has always tried to be like Gil—throwing a football, catching a pass, making a touchdown—a big guy among big guys who always treat him like a dog.

We were passing Mom's cottonwoods when Ed started to moan. We stopped talking then, because once he began to moan he didn't stop. His moans rose to wails, and built beyond that until he was shrieking, his eyes closed all the while. Charlie stuck his fingers in his ears. Ruth shut her eyes and clapped her hands over her mouth as if to hold back screams. I bit my lip until I broke the skin and tasted blood like iron. Only Gil seemed unaffected, all his attention trained on driving. He leaned into the wheel; he gripped it so hard his knuckles went white.

We turned down the road that led to the hospital, and finally pulled up in front of the emergency room. When the car stopped moving, Ed stopped screaming. He'd fainted again.

"Let's drop him off and get the hell out of here," Charlie said.

I looked at Charlie for what felt like the first time. Something inside me turned cold and hard and weighty as a stone.

"Some friend," I said.

Gil snapped, "One of you girls, go get help."

"One of us girls," Ruth repeated. I couldn't begin to imagine what was going on inside of her.

"Yeah. What about it?" Gil twisted around in the seat. Sweat trickled down his forehead. "I can't leave my car."

Ruth started to laugh, and then she couldn't stop. She couldn't seem to get out of the car.

"Shut the fuck up!" Charlie yelled.

"You're jostling him!" Gil snapped as I slipped from beneath Ed.

I practically spoke gibberish to the ER nurse; still she nodded and strode off toward the front desk. I ran back outside and was surprised to see Charlie present and accounted for, pacing by the entrance. Gil was leaning over the seat, talking reassuringly to Ed; he was stroking Ed's damp hair. Ruth still held Ed's feet. She'd stopped laughing, at least. I started toward the car, but Charlie grabbed my hand.

"Don't say anything," he said. "Don't let on you know what happened. We found Ed, that's all. We found him on the beach." Charlie slid his arm around my waist and pulled me close. I swayed against him. "We don't know anything," Charlie whispered. "We wanted to help, that's all. This could be Ed's fault. Actually, it *is* his fault, isn't it? He should have known better." Charlie nuzzled my ear.

I stepped away and looked into Charlie's green eyes. They were wide with innocence.

"You're cool, right?" he said.

I said, "I don't think so."

Just then, orderlies rushed out with a gurney. They heaved Ed onto it and whisked him inside and out of sight. Gil and Ruth joined Charlie and me by the entrance. For a moment, we just stood there, silent.

"I'll park the car," Gil said slowly.

I nodded like a dumb animal. "I'll go in."

Charlie said, "Do what you want, but *I'm* getting out of here."

"Wait." I held out my hand to Charlie, but he was already running away. I looked at my hand in the air. Sand crusted my nails. I could smell lake water in my hair.

"Chicken shit," Ruth yelled at Charlie.

She and I went into the waiting room. We sat in hard, orange chairs. Gil joined us there. I was so tired all of a sudden. I wanted Mom's arms around me.

Ruth, Gil, and I waited in the ER for maybe half an hour. There didn't seem to be anything we needed to say to one another. Finally, Ruth gave me a poke in the ribs. A tall, gangly doctor was headed our way. He stopped in front of us and took off his glasses. Rubbing his eyes, he quietly asked us what had happened.

In a shaky voice, Ruth told the doctor everything. "It was my fault," she said. "I brought the fireworks." She told the doctor her name, and then she looked at Gil and me. We sounded nice and polite, introducing ourselves.

The doctor raised his eyebrows. "'Gil Perez,' as in Troy City Trojans?"

Gil sat up a little straighter and nodded. He looked at me. "Her dad is the coach."

The doctor didn't seem to hear. "The nurse said there was a fourth guy?"

"Besides Ed, you mean?" Gil said.

The doctor nodded. Waited.

"Charlie Wates was there, too," Gil finally said.

"I'm going to have to report *this* to the police." The doctor put his glasses back on. "Your friend's lucky he isn't blind. He's lucky he has all his fingers."

"But he's going to be okay?" Gil asked.

"I wouldn't say he's going to be okay. He's got third-degree burns. He'll live, if that's what you mean, but for a while, it's not going to be easy."

"But—" I remembered Ed's trumpet, lifted toward the sky. "He needs his hands."

"Who doesn't?" The doctor turned to go. Then he looked back at us. "That boy's parents will be here any minute. Pick another day to make your apologies."

"We should leave?" Gil said.

"You should leave," the doctor said.

The three of us drifted outside. Ruth immediately headed off across the parking lot.

Gil pulled his keys from his pocket. "Where is she going?"

"Her house, probably. She lives close enough to walk."

"Do you?"

I shook my head.

"Get in," Gil ordered, and he drove me home.

On the way, he said one other thing. "If your dad asks about me, tell him I know what we did was wrong."

JULY 8

Hands. Big, rough hands like Dad's, passing a football. Delicate, manicured hands like Mom's, braiding
dark hair like mine. Stubby, quick hands like Ruth's,
thumbing through catalogs and racks of clothes.
Strong, tanned hands like Charlie's buttoning and
unbuttoning shirts, shorts, and jeans. But no freckled hands, like Ed's, playing the trumpet.

*F*our weeks community service. That's what Gil,
Charlie, and Ruth got. Four weeks community service for
abusing illegal substances—fireworks, not grain alcohol,
which, I found out, was what Gil's little flask held. Four
weeks community service for disrupting the peace on a
Sunday morning. Four weeks that end exactly the day
before Gil heads off to Michigan State. This was decided
yesterday in Sheriff Byrne's office, not twenty-four hours

after Ed entered the hospital. Ruth, Charlie, and Gil were called into the police station to hear their sentences.

"It won't go on our records, not this one time," Ruth told me on the phone early this morning. "Everyone in this stupid town wants Gil to make a name for us at M.S.U. next year. Just like everyone wants Charlie to make a name for us right here at home. And everyone knows I'm Pastor Bob's kid. For his sake, I get to keep my pristine reputation."

"What about me?" I asked.

Ruth's laugh was harsh. "Oh, you? Livy, you have nothing to worry about. You can bask in the sun for the rest of the summer."

My throat tightened. "What do you mean?"

"Sheriff Byrne basically said that he'd already dealt with you. You don't need a harder time than the one you're already having, he said. Plus, he's best buds with your dad, right? A real Trojans fan? I'm sure he doesn't want to upset Coach any more than Coach is already upset. If that were to happen, we might not have a winning season next year! I bet Sheriff Byrne didn't even tell your dad."

I didn't say that Dad knew everything; I was sure of it. I didn't say he wouldn't look at me or speak to me. I didn't say it's like I don't exist; I'm not his problem. I didn't say I'd rather be doing time that comes to an end.

"I'm sorry," I said.

"*You're* sorry? *I'm* grounded forever. When I'm not serving the community, I'm serving at home. Slaving at home, I mean."

"It's not fair—"

But Ruth had already hung up. I stood in the kitchen, listening to the dial tone. Four weeks community service was tough—washing windows, collecting litter, cleaning up graffiti, scouring public toilets. But they could do those things—Ruth, Gil and Charlie. *We* could do those things. We had hands.

The teakettle's whistle shrilled, and I turned off the burner. I was boiling water to clean Mom's humidifier. I lifted the kettle, then clunked it back on the stove and ran for the sink. I thought I was going to be sick. Something spattered on the hot range smelled like Ed's burned hands.

I would find Dad, I decided. I would tell him Sheriff Byrne had to see me. I needed to be punished, too.

I went to the living room, where I knew Dad would be. And he was. He was sitting beside Mom, who was actually awake, propped up on pillows in bed. Her mouth was closed tight, a thin line of resistance.

"Please try," Dad was saying. He lifted a spoon in the air. Balanced precariously on his lap was a tray, and balanced precariously on the tray was a bowl of chicken soup. "Just one spoonful, Gracie."

Mom shook her head fiercely. Dad lowered the spoon into the bowl and stared into the soup like he could see his future there. Then he sighed, lifted up another brimming spoonful, blew on it, and moved it slowly toward Mom's mouth.

"It's not too hot," Dad said. "I promise."

Mom made a low sound in her throat—almost a growl—and waved her hand at the spoon as if to bat it away. And she almost did. She almost knocked the spoon from Dad's grip. Dad's eyes narrowed. He got a look I've seen him get when a football player like Charlie acts up—a look of rage controlled by sheer will.

"You have to eat," Dad spoke softly through clenched teeth. He leaned over Mom. He held her head with one hand and pushed the spoon against her lips, trying to pry her mouth open. Mom tried to shake her head, but Dad held her head still. I looked away. Then bowl and tray clattered to the floor, and someone was crying. I looked up. Dad was crying. The soup was a puddle at his feet.

I picked up the bowl and spoon and set them on the tray. My stomach churned at the smell of the soup. It looked awful there on the floor, like something toxic that shouldn't be eaten.

"I have to go now." Dad could barely speak. His face was wet with tears. "Tell her I'll be back soon."

"Tell me yourself," Mom whispered, but Dad ran from the room. Mom and I listened to him leave the house; we listened as the car pulled out of the driveway.

"Mom?" I finally said. She stared out the window. There was a red mark on her lower lip where the spoon had pressed. The mark reminded me of Ed's callus.

For a moment, the room seemed to spin. I shook my head, trying to clear it. Then I saw the soup splashed on Mom's neck. I gently wiped the soup away.

"What can I do?" I said.

Mom tried to smile. The red mark on her lip went white. "He never asks what he can do anymore." Her voice was hoarse. "He just does. Like people just do when they're barely surviving."

I looked again at the mess on the floor. Bile rose in my throat. But I said, "Maybe he's right, though? Maybe you should eat something?"

"I can't swallow," Mom said. "Your dad won't believe it, but I *can't*." She arched her neck and moaned, "I'm hungry and I can't eat," as if God above might hear her and help.

I ran to the kitchen, grabbed a tray of ice chips from the freezer, and ran back to the living room. "I can't," Mom was saying. Then she saw the ice tray in my hand and opened her mouth like a baby bird. I placed an ice chip on her tongue. She closed her eyes and was quiet for some time, sucking on the ice, letting it soothe her. She savored that chip and then another, like ice had all the nutrients she'd ever need—vitamins and minerals, protein and carbohydrates, to carry her from this day to the next.

The red mark on Mom's lower lip had risen to a little welt. I pried another ice chip from the tray and stroked it back and forth over the welt, over her dry lips. Gradually, the ice melted. Water ran down her chin, dripped into the deep hollow at the base of her throat. Mom gave a small sound of pleasure, and I pried out another chip. I worked my way through five. I could feel the cold in my fingers, below my skin, at my bones.

"Enough," Mom finally said.

"There's plenty more," I said urgently. This was what Dad must feel, I thought. This desperation to *do* for her.

Mom pointed at the radiator beneath the window. "There."

I looked at the radiator. On it lay her Bible.

"Read to me?" Mom asked.

She sounded like me, little, asking for a story.

Suddenly, my heart was racing. I wanted to do for her the way *I* wanted to do for her. I said, "Are you sure you don't want something to eat?"

She looked at me until I finally went and got the Bible. The dusty black cover was ringed with sticky circles from medicine bottles. I picked it up, thumbed through the thin pages. Some of them were crisp and crinkled with coffee stains.

"A psalm," Mom said.

I found the Book of Psalms in the index and skimmed a few. They all seemed angry and warlike, not peaceful at all. Where, I wondered, was the Lord-is-my-shepherd one, the one Mom used to read to me when I was little? That was the kind of psalm I wanted now—all still waters and green pastures, with only a quick mention of shadows, evil, and dark valleys of death.

"One thirty-nine," Mom said.

I looked up from the Bible.

"One, three, nine," Mom said firmly. "One hundred and thirty-nine."

I finally found the page, dog-eared at the bottom corner. *Nasty habit. I don't want to see you doing this. Never ever.* Mom's voice in my head—her other voice, not frail like now. The psalm was long. My sigh sounded too loud. Quickly, I started reading.

"'O Lord, Thou hast searched me and known me.'"

I read on, trying to understand what was being said. But the verses didn't come out like whole thoughts, they came out like fragments—a puzzle of words that I couldn't put together at first, each piece a separate unit, divided from the others. "Flee," I read, and "overwhelm." Then I started reading about darkness and light. I could imagine darkness and light, like a picture of the first day of creation in a Sunday-school book, and that helped me understand the next part:

> "For Thou didst form my inward parts;
> Thou didst weave me in my mother's womb.
> I will give thanks to Thee, for I am fearfully
> and wonderfully made."

I stopped reading. I stared at the words.

"Go on," Mom said.

I took a breath, and continued:

> "My frame was not hidden from Thee,
> When I was made in secret,
> And skillfully wrought in the depths of the earth.
> And in Thy book they were all written,
> The days that were ordained for me. . . ."

The words swam before my eyes. There were only a few more verses to go. The rest of the psalm was mostly about slaying the wicked, the kind of stuff I hadn't wanted to read before, but was glad to read now. Biblical bloodshed was safer than Mom and me in a room that suddenly felt too small. I opened my mouth to read, but Mom grasped my hand.

"Did you hear it?" She searched my face, her eyes pleading. She seemed to see nothing in my face that she wanted to see. I could feel how set my expression was; I could feel how I looked like Dad. Mom swallowed several times, or tried to. She needs ice, I thought. I looked at the tray. In the heat, only a few slivers remained, floating in water. All the windows in the room were open, but there wasn't a breeze; the curtains hung perfectly still.

I stood up from the bed. "You want the fan on?"

"You were made in me," Mom said. "Wonderfully made."

I went and put the Bible back on the radiator.

"I was wonderfully made, too," she said. "Once."

I looked out the window. "You still are."

"Still?"

I didn't move.

"Come here," Mom said.

"I think there's more soup if you want it."

"Livy."

I stood at the window for as long as I could. When I finally sat down on the bed again, Mom put her hand to my cheek. Her thin hand passed like a shadow over my face. She said something I could barely hear. "Beautiful," I think she said.

Then she started to cough, and she couldn't stop. She wasn't breathing. She wasn't breathing at all. She clung to my arm, her mouth open, her eyes bulging. Mrs. Ford, I thought. I tried to pull away to call Mrs. Ford. But Mom was stronger. She held on for dear life.

I remembered the oxygen. I put the mask on Mom and switched on the tank. In a moment, Mom had air; she was breathing, then quiet, exhausted. When her eyes closed, she let go of my arm. That's when I ran and phoned Mrs. Ford. I had seen her earlier, trimming the holly bushes that border her house, making them neat, making them even, pruning them back so her children can play safely around thorns. She came right away. She took one look at Mom and called an ambulance. When the ambulance arrived, siren blaring, Mrs. Ford told me that she would ride with Mom to the hospital. She said that she'd be able to fill the doctors in on Mom's situation. "You stay here and get some rest," she said. "Take care of yourself."

Will you at least take care of yourself? I thought, as I

JULY 13

A jumble of pieces. An Austrian cowbell. A painted shack floating on a calm lake. The tapered leaves of a weeping willow. Curls and tendrils that could only be Ruth's. Ed's hands whole, poised on the trumpet, then raw as meat. Mom's mouth, the welt on her lip. Her eyes, wide and dark as a deer's. Dad, a shadow at the door.

One puzzle after the next, jagged and broken. And none of the pieces fit.

*I*n the last few days, waiting to see Mom, I've put together the Eiffel Tower, a deer in a forest, and a hot-air balloon in a blue sky. Community service is sounding better all the time. But it's not going to happen. Dad wants me at the hospital, it's clear. I'm grounded—just not at home.

Today, I started on the Statue of Liberty. She's the biggest puzzle I've tried. Her one thousand pieces have gone soft with age, and they smell of mildew, like the pages of *Gone with the Wind*. I've been sitting at the same wobbly table every day. It's tucked into a corner of the solarium, next to big windows. The sun streams in there. It brightens the puzzle pieces and covers me like a comforter. When it's sunny. Today was cloudy. The gray sky seemed to hang right at the treetops; the wind blew so hard, the windows rattled. There was a summer storm brewing and it hadn't let loose yet. All day, the air seemed electric with waiting. Everyone talked about the weather—doctors, nurses, visitors—everyone stopped what they were doing to stare out the windows and say, "Look at that sky! Boy, the temperature sure has dropped!"

It's as low as it can go now, surely. Downright cold, and dusk. I'm home, sitting on the front porch, listening to fat drops of rain hit the earth like the ground has done something wrong. I'm writing out in the open where anyone can see me, if anyone was stupid enough to walk beneath a sky that's turned the color of old, hard-boiled egg yolk. You'd think a sky like this would smell like sulfur. I keep holding my breath against a rotten smell that isn't there. Still, there's life out here—things alive, riding out the storm in the trees and grass—which makes out here better than my empty house.

When I saw Mom today, I talked about the

weather, too. She'd just woken up; she was about ready to sleep again. She was writhing on the bed. Today, like every other day, I saw Mom briefly, once in the morning and once in the afternoon. She might be awake more than that, but I don't know; I'm not there. Doctor's orders, I guess, or Dad's. Sometimes I think it tires Mom to see me at all.

"It's cold in here too, kind of, isn't it? Cold like outside." That's what I could think of to say today. Mom tapped her covers. I saw that Dad had put two more blankets on top of her usual one. "You warm enough?" I asked, taking her hand. But Mom was already asleep.

I went back to my wobbly table to work on the Statue of Liberty. My head ached, and I couldn't figure out why. Maybe, I thought, because I was worried that some of the statue's puzzle pieces might be missing. There had been no French flag for the top of the Eiffel Tower, no white belly for the brown deer. There was a hole in the hot-air balloon where a bit of gray tabletop showed through.

By noon I had pieced together the statue's head, from her crown to her neck—no missing pieces yet. I worked on her hands, then. They looked like a football player's hands, like Dad's hands. I looked at my hands. They're completely different from the statue's or Dad's; they're exactly like

Mom's—long and thin, with tapered nails, the most grace-ful thing about me. Mom used to say I could borrow her jewelry someday, for special occasions. "I can't wait to see you all dressed up for the prom," Mom used to say. "My emerald ring and gold bracelet on your hands." I gazed into the statue's eyes—dead eyes, zombie eyes. Then I swung my arm across the wobbly table and swept the puz-zle pieces to the floor. I had to get out of the solarium.

I took the elevator down to the lobby, thinking I'd wait outside for Dad. I'd wait outside through the worst storm. Instead, I found myself standing at the front desk.

"Is Ed Allen still a patient here?" I asked the recep-tionist.

She leafed through a card catalogue, then looked up at me over her reading glasses and smiled. "You'd better hurry. He's going home today." She handed me the famil-iar pink visitor's pass. "Room 347A. That's the third floor, you know."

I knew. Every day since Mom's been in the hos-pital, I've walked by Ed's room at least once. I've been too afraid to go in, especially since his parents are always there, talking or reading aloud to Ed.

This is your last chance to do the right thing, I thought, as the elevator lurched to a stop on the third floor. I walked to Ed's room at the end of the hall. The door was open, but I knocked anyway. When nobody answered, I peered inside.

Ed was alone, standing at the window, his back to me. The last time I'd really seen him was just before the nurses rushed him into the ER. He'd looked so frail lying there on the gurney. Now, standing before the window, staring out at the cloudy sky and wind-tossed trees, he didn't look frail at all. He was standing straight, and his shoulders looked somehow broader.

I took a few steps into his room and my knees buckled. I grabbed the back of a chair to keep from falling.

Ed turned, his bandaged hands raised in the air like boxing gloves. Beneath the fluorescent light the white strips of gauze seemed to glow. Watching me, he slowly lowered his hands.

"What are you doing here?" he said.

"Um." I braced myself against the chair. "How are you doing?"

Ed shrugged.

"Hanging in there?" I asked.

"You tell me."

I was rubbing my hands together, I realized, like they ached. I clasped them. "I don't know."

"Neither do I. You're here, why don't you come on in?"

"Thanks," I said. "Thanks." I went and stood by Ed at the window. He didn't say anything and I couldn't think of what to say, so I told him Mom was in the hospital, too. I didn't tell him why, or that it was bad this time, that it might be the last time. But I told him she was there, one floor down, sick.

Ed looked at me and I looked out the window, at the clouds that wouldn't burst. Ed looked out the window too, and then, for a while, like everyone else today, we talked about the weather.

Then Ed said, "There's my folks."

He pointed at a man and a woman coming up the sidewalk to the hospital entrance. The man was tall and slight, like Ed, with Ed's thick, sandy hair. Ed's plump, blond mother didn't look so much like him, but she moved like him. She darted and wavered, more than walked. As we watched, she stopped short and bowed her head. Ed's dad took her in his arms.

"It's hardest on them." Ed sat on the bed. He drew his breath in sharply through his teeth. "Skin grafting. They took it off my legs. Hurt like hell for the first week, but it's getting better now. Won't hurt at all, I guess, in another week or so. But, still sometimes, if I hit it just right—" He shook his head. "I just have to be careful."

What could I say? I told him I was sorry, then looked

back out the window. The man and the woman were gone.

"They're on their way up," I said.

"Here we go." Ed sighed. "I think they would have cut off their own hands rather than have this happen to me. Especially my mom."

"I'm sorry," I said again.

"They keep trying to be brave. They keep trying to pretend that nothing's wrong, that everything's all right." Ed laughed bitterly. "Even when the doctor said that I probably won't be able to use my hands for much for a while, they tried to act cheery. They said we'd go to the best clinics. I'd be as good as new. Okay. I want to go to the best clinics. But I'll never be as good as new. My mother is going to spend every spare moment she's got crying, thinking I can't see her. That'll drive me crazy. At first I thought these hands would drive me crazy. But she will, he will, if I let them."

Ed sat up a little straighter on the bed. "There they are—I'd know my mom's footsteps anywhere. Listen to her. The only thing that she's sure of is that she's a *wreck*." Ed was breathing hard. "Did you know I have—I *had*—as much of a chance for a college music scholarship as Gil had for a sports scholarship? I'll be able to play the trumpet again someday, if everything goes all right, the doctor said. But a scholarship? I doubt it."

"Hi, honey!" Ed's mom stood in the doorway, smiling, her blue eyes bright with tears.

Ed stood up from the bed. He opened his arms. His mom scurried over to him and held him close. His father hovered nearby, patting Ed on the shoulder.

"I've said it before and I'll say it again," Ed's dad said. "The food here agrees with you. You look healthy as a horse."

Ed looked at his dad, and his dad blinked and looked at me.

"Who's this?"

"A friend," Ed said. "Livy Moore."

Ed's mom drew in a breath through her teeth. "Coach Moore's daughter?"

Ed nodded. His parents looked at me without smiling. I took a step back. Then another.

"So you have the courtesy to pay a visit," Ed's dad said.

"Gil and Jackie came," Ed said. "Remember? The flowers?"

"Oh, yeah." Ed's dad sighed. "The least they could do, right? The very least."

"Bye, Ed." I started for the door. I wanted to run, fast and far, into the storm.

"Wait," Ed said.

I stopped. His parents were watching me.

"I'm not doing much the next few weeks, except some killer rehab exercises. Picking up pencils. Squeezing rubber balls. Things like that." Ed did a few cautious arm curls. "If you get bored, give me a call, okay?"

I nodded.

In the lobby, Dad was standing by the revolving door, watching the darkening sky. I went to him.

"It's so cold," he said, pressing his hand against the glass.

He led me to the car. We needed to get back to the house and close the storm windows, he said. Mom was expecting him back after that, but I could stay home if I wanted.

I wanted. Especially after Dad told me the nurse's prediction: this might be a long night for Mom. Dad was planning on spending it with her.

"Who's that?" Dad asked as we slowed to a stop in front of our house. He pounded his fist on the car horn. "Whose beater is that, blocking our driveway?"

Charlie hopped out of an old, yellow car and started toward us, a grin plastered on his face. Without thinking, I sank down in my seat. Luckily, Dad didn't seem to notice. "Move it!" he was yelling, louder than necessary.

"Yes, sure, sorry, sir," Charlie called, trotting back to his car. He pulled out into the street, then pulled back in behind us. Dad and I got out, and Dad gave Charlie a once-over.

"What do you want?" Dad asked.

Charlie stopped short. He was still grinning, but it looked like work. "Um, I thought maybe you could give me some advice about preseason training? I want to be ready for fall, now that Gil's graduated. My throwing arm's a little weak."

Dad started for the house. "I hear you've been doing some training already. Throwing fireworks."

Charlie's grin failed him. He trotted after Dad, brushing against me as he passed.

"Listen," Dad said, fitting his key into the front door, "the less I see of you now, the less I'll remember you in the fall. And I know there's some things you're hoping I'll forget. So why don't you get smart and get out of here?" Dad opened the door and stepped inside. He looked at me through the screen. "Remember, you're grounded, Livy," he said, before he turned and disappeared into the house.

I waited for Dad to tell me to get inside. I *wanted* Dad to tell me to get inside. He didn't. So I straightened my spine and faced Charlie.

"You're grounded." Charlie smirked, his face a mask

of pity. "Guess that means you can't join me over at Goodlove. Scrubbing out johns."

"Guess not."

Charlie nodded. He crossed his arms over his chest. "You tell your dad about us?"

I shook my head, my cheeks burning.

"Huh. Looks like you'd rather he didn't know."

"What do you think?"

"Sounds like a good idea to me. But sometimes I let things slip out, you know? By accident. What I'm thinking is, why don't you make sure your dad knows I'm a really good guy. A true friend. And I won't let him know what kind of friends we actually were for a trillionth of a second. Okay?" Charlie smiled, but his eyes weren't friendly.

I tried to laugh. "Sounds like blackmail."

"You've been watching way too much TV."

"Yeah, right. Like after-school specials. There was this one where a kid treats everyone like shit when he's seventeen. A few years later he's on the streets."

Charlie shrugged. "Sounds tragic."

"So what do you think you'll be doing when you're twenty?"

"What I have to," Charlie said, and he stalked to his car.

JULY 16

God, please. No more puzzle dreams.

For the fourth night in a row, Dad dropped me off at home after another day at the solarium, then drove off to spend the night with Mom. This time when I went into the dim, silent house, I stood for way too long looking at the empty hospital bed. I sat down on the thing; I started to lie down on it. Then I smelled Mom in the pillow. I ran to the kitchen. I grabbed the phone book, looked up Ed's number, and dialed it.

Ed answered. He didn't sound surprised to hear from me. His voice kept getting muffled; he seemed to be having a hard time holding the phone to his ear. Suddenly, he dropped the phone with a clatter. After a whispered exchange with his dad, Ed picked up the phone again and said that he could do something right then, if I wanted.

"Like what?" I asked.

"I don't know, exactly. But I was talking with Ruth's dad the other day—"

"Pastor Bob?" I blurted out. "You don't even go to his church."

Ed was quiet for a moment. "He visited me a few times at the hospital. Ruth was too ashamed to come, he said, and he felt too badly about what happened to me to stay away. Anyway, we've been talking some. And he said I should think about visiting Goodlove. Soon."

Goodlove was the last place I wanted to go. I didn't want to see the lake or the beach. It was too late in the day for Charlie to be working, but for all I knew, there might be some remains left behind from the explosion. Scraps of Ed's skin or chunks of his flesh. I shuddered.

"I can't drive," Ed said.

"Oh. Yeah. Of course. And I don't have a car."

"What about the Firebird?"

I sat down on a kitchen chair. The clock ticked

loudly above the sink. "How do you know about that?"

"Everyone knows about *that*. We all lust after it."

"It's not my car. It's my mom's. I've never even driven it."

"Okay. Just a thought. Well, maybe we could meet here, then? It's a long walk, I know, but what if you took your bike?"

When I told him that my bike was trashed, Ed went and asked his dad for a ride to my house. A few minutes later, he returned to the phone to tell me that his dad had refused. "He's too busy," Ed explained. I tried to believe this.

But it didn't matter anyway. Because I'd been doing some thinking while Ed was away from the phone. I'd been thinking about me spending another night alone in an empty house. I'd been thinking about Ed, alone, too. I'd been thinking about the sleek red convertible in the garage. The keys in Mom's jewelry box. And I'd been thinking that if Mom had known what I was about to do, she probably would have said okay. "Have fun," she probably would have said.

"You think Goodlove would be fun?" I asked Ed.

"No. Therapeutic, maybe."

"I'm grounded," I said. "For the first time ever."

"Do you care?"

"Not really."

"Why don't you tell your dad that I begged you to set me free? Tell him that I had to escape or my hands would fall off. Blame it on me."

I said, "I could probably use some therapy, too."

I took Mom's keys from the dusty box on her dresser, trying not to look at the jewelry inside. I ran downstairs to the garage and lifted the heavy metal door. I stood by the Firebird for a moment, my eyes adjusting. When the car materialized in the ash-gray shadows, I gasped. I'd forgotten how beautiful it was.

It took me a while to settle into the red leather seat. I kept adjusting its position, only to realize that I was taller than Mom now. I breathed in the faint scent of her rose perfume. I ran my hands around the steering wheel. Finally, I fit the key into the ignition. I turned the key, and the engine roared to life, its throaty rumble reverberating off the garage walls. I shifted into reverse and backed into the driveway. Then I sailed away from the house and toward Ed. This car was made for me, I thought, and I had to pull off by some cornfields to catch my breath. "I didn't mean that," I said, to the sun visor, the speedometer, the glove compartment stuffed with Mom's map, flashlight, and box of tissues. "I didn't mean that at all." Then I pulled back onto the road.

Ed lives in a house that looks like mine plopped down in another subdivision. He was waiting on the front porch when I turned into the driveway. I leaned across the seat and opened the door for him. He didn't wave his bandaged hands at his mother, who stood at their kitchen window watching. Her plump shoulders slumped as we drove away.

"I don't really want to open the windows or put down the top," I said. It smells like my mom in here, I didn't say.

Ed raised his eyebrows, but then shrugged. "Okay by me."

We didn't talk much for a few miles. We were driving down Cottonwood Lane when I asked, "Are you sure you want to do this?" Ed nodded. I tried to keep my mind on the car, not the destination. I tried not to glance at Ed's bandages, which was difficult since he kept moving his hands. He'd cradle one in the other, switching back and forth every few minutes. He couldn't seem to get comfortable. A couple of times, he brought his hands to his mouth and adjusted the strips of gauze with his teeth.

Ed started whispering to himself as we turned into the forest preserve. We parked in the sandy lot. When I turned off the car, I could make out Ed's words. "Dream on, dream on, dream on," he whispered. Then he went quiet. We sat for a while, listening to the engine tick. It was dusk now. Cars packed with couples kept pulling in beside us. Hand in hand, the couples took off down the narrow trail to the beach.

"You want the radio on?" I finally asked.

Ed shook his head. "If you can't beat 'em," he said, nodding to some kids kicking through the sand. I opened the door for him and he got out of the car.

I made sure the Firebird was locked, even though that's not the kind of thing you do around here, then looked up to see Ed walking quickly down the trail. I ran after him, the keys weighty in my pocket. By the time I reached the beach, Ed had kicked off his shoes. He was standing in shallow water. He skimmed his foot across the surface and said, "I don't even remember where it happened, do you?"

"No," I lied. I was standing not ten feet away from where the M-80 went off. Ed was silent, watching the waves.

"People stake out claims here, kind of. At least, that's what Ruth used to tell me," I said. And then I started blabbing on, trying to fill up the quiet. "The earlier you get here, or the later, the better a spot you'll get—one that's secluded but has a nice view. Most important, it should have a comfortable patch of ground. Clean sand. That's what everyone looks for. Only, there's a lot of stones, aren't there? And glass. I never noticed all the glass before, and litter. You'd think they could keep it cleaner." I thought of Charlie working here during the day. I kicked off my shoes and went to stand beside Ed. The shallow water felt warm.

Ed chopped the water with his heel. "So let's go look for someplace comfortable."

Uh-oh, I thought, and started to shake my head, but Ed had already started for the shore, so I followed him. Carefully, still wary of the skin on his thighs, he sat down on the sand. I plopped down, too. We sat there, side by side, like friends, nothing else. A white sliver of moon hung low in the sky. I raised my hand and covered the moon with my thumb. My fingers spanned the distance to the setting sun, smeared orange across the horizon.

"Ruth's right." Ed gestured to a nearby sandbar, where cattails rustled vigorously. "The joint is jumping."

We laughed. It felt good, laughing like that with Ed.

After a while, we scooted down to the wet sand and dipped our feet back into the water. Little minnows nibbled our toes. The sun sank out of sight, and the sky darkened. We watched the moon's reflection breaking and mending again on the waves. Occasionally, a kid would tear past us, laughing, or not, chased by another kid, or not. Stars appeared, glimmering to life.

Ed pointed at one bright, fixed fleck. "That's Venus, I think. You can usually count on her. Even when the rest of the sky looks empty."

"My mom," I said. I tried again, "My mom—"

On the sandbar, cattails stirred. A girl rose up there. She was wearing a bikini top and shorts, and her skin glowed milky white in the moonlight. She stretched her arms toward the sky and yawned. Someone grabbed at her belt. She batted the person's hand away and turned her face toward the stars. But the hand pulled her down.

Ed gave a low whistle. "That's Ruth."

I looked at him quickly. His face was serious. "How do you know?"

"Her hair. How many people have short, curly hair like that? And besides, I have developed an eye for the female form. To me, it's like stargazing. I can pick out unique characteristics and—"

"Right." My heart was racing.

"Right." Ed laughed, then he studied my expression and got serious. "Who is she with, I wonder. Not Gil, that's for sure. At the hospital, Gil told me he'd had enough of high school girls. Boy, if Pastor Bob could see his little girl now."

I wasn't cold, but I shivered. "Maybe I should go check on her?"

We sat quietly for a moment, listening to the cattails rustle.

"I'm going to check on her," I said.

At that moment, Ruth stood up again. Swatting cattails aside, she crossed the sandbar to the shore. A lanky guy in swim trunks scrambled after her.

"That's Tom Lazarus," Ed said.

Ed was right. The guy was Tom, no doubt about it—all skin and bone and wiry muscle, with a couple of tattoos thrown in for good measure. I groaned as Ruth bent down to brush sand from her legs, and Tom stumbled and fell at her feet. Ed gave me a quick look. "Maybe she likes him because he's got such a religious last name—you know, like Lazarus from the Bible? Who got raised from the dead?"

Ed was talking in questions like he used to. Maybe, I thought, Ed talked in questions when he felt anxious. Because I sure felt anxious—for Ruth. Tom Lazarus is supposedly a genius, with an IQ that's off the charts. Tom is also about as burned out as a burnout can get. He was supposed to graduate this past year, but he never made it through fall term. He dropped out, then stumbled from job to job. Ruth told me this herself. The rumor is— Ruth told me—Tom spends most of his time hanging out at one of the seedier bars in Troy City, wasting his brain, drinking it soggy. Tom's wasting his looks, too. He was handsome once upon a time, tall and dark-haired, with blue eyes that, once upon a time, you might have called "piercing." Those eyes are watery and red now. His hair is lank and dirty. And he's not so tall when he stands hunched over the way he does.

I got a good look at Tom when I jumped up, shook off Ed's hand and his warning look, and dashed across the sand to Ruth.

"Hey, Livy," she said casually, when I reached her side, panting. It was almost like she was expecting me. Then she looked over my shoulder and saw Ed, and her face tightened. "Is he okay?"

"He's okay." I looked down at Tom, sitting spaced out in the sand. "Is he?"

"Same as he ever was." Ruth poked her toe in Tom's ribs, and Tom grunted. "He's got a car. He's got beer. He doesn't mind late nights, which is the only time I've got to call my own."

"I thought you were grounded."

Ruth laughed. "I thought *you* were grounded."

"Touché," I said, and we kind of smiled at each other. But then I made the mistake of saying, "I guess you're dating Tom now?"

Ruth's expression hardened. "Don't tell me you're turning into a snob, Livy."

"Ruth—"

She pushed past me and went over to Ed. She rested her hand on his shoulder. "I've been wanting to tell you—" Ruth caught her breath. She tried again. "I'm sorry."

When Ed nodded, Ruth walked back to Tom. She pulled Tom to his feet, saying, "Come on, get up, I've got to go home. I've got to work tomorrow."

Smiling sweetly, Tom turned and walked right into the lake. He kept walking until the water reached his waist, then he floated on his back. Ruth looked tired, watching Tom. But she went into the water after him. She guided him back to shore, and past me.

I followed Ruth to Tom's car. She didn't tell me to beat it, even though I was right on her heels. When she struggled to open the back door, I said, "I'll get it," and did. Then I helped her lay Tom down on the backseat.

"We keep doing this," I said. "We keep helping boys into cars."

"Lucky us." Ruth got into the front seat and started the car.

I wasn't ready to give up on her yet. I leaned in through her open window and bumped my forehead against hers. "Hey, you. Anybody home?"

Ruth held up her hands. Her palms were covered with blisters. "Lawn mower," she said. "I don't mind, really. It hurts, breaking in my skin. But it's good work, cutting grass and pruning and weeding. Every day my boss tells me that I'm helping Troy City look good. The problem is, I hate Troy City. I hate this place. I envy Gil getting out. And Jackie—she'll get out too. She's so smart. Even Charlie will get out. He's not a great athlete, and he's not smart, but he'll do what he has to." I must have reacted to this, because Ruth nodded. "I bet you've heard him say that at least once or twice. I know I sure have. So where does that leave me? I don't know. But I've got to get out of here. For the last few months, I've been feeling that way more and more. You've been so checked out, you might as well have been away. But don't you wish you were really gone sometimes? Don't you wish you were out of here?"

I shrugged. "It hasn't really been an option."

"You have to make your own options, make your own choices. Exercise your free will. That's one thing my dad has taught me." Ruth frowned and jammed a key into the ignition. "Judge not, lest ye be judged. Dad taught me that, too. In Sunday school, remember? And there was another thing we learned, too. Something like: Shake the dust off your sandals and beat it. Remember that one? Straight from Jesus' mouth to our ears."

"I remember." I studied Ruth's face, glowing palely in the moonlight. There were heavy shadows beneath her eyes.

"I'm not dating Tom," she said. "I'm exercising my free will."

When we started high school, Ruth always used to talk about "discovering herself." She planned on doing it in college. She would discover herself there, she said, then she would pursue her dreams until she'd lived them. Maybe she'd travel the world. Maybe she'd get her PhD in something she couldn't even begin to imagine. Maybe she'd be a politician or a war correspondent. Then maybe she would be ready for Him, the Man of her Dreams. *Maybe.* Or maybe she'd stay single, like Joan of Arc, Queen Elizabeth, Marie Curie, Helen Keller—all those saints, artists, scholars, and queens, who didn't have space for a man or a family, whose biographies we had devoured. There was strength to be gained, Ruth said to me once, when a woman lived this way, "Not like the women in Troy City," she said. "You mean, women like our moms?" I asked, and Ruth said, "You got it."

"Don't look at me like that, Livy," Ruth said now. She started to roll up the car window.

"I'm worried." I put my hands on the window.

But Ruth forced it all the way up, saying, "Worry about yourself."

I watched her car's taillights until they shrank to small red stars on the horizon, then flickered and disappeared altogether. Standing there, I remembered Ed's mom, watching at the window, looking so worried, so left behind. "Pathetic," I said to nobody, about nobody in particular. And then I went back to Ed.

JULY 23

I'm trying to help a boy into the Firebird. He turns on me, glaring.

"I can take care of myself."

The boy has Dad's weathered face. That new, dense, silvery patch in his bangs.

We were passing each other on the stairs when Dad told me. Sometimes we can't help but do things like that—pass each other—even though we're hardly ever together. But there I was, halfway down the stairs, and there was Dad, determined to come up, and there we were facing each other. Dad looked at me and said, "Your mother is coming home tomorrow. She's coming home for good."

"For good," I repeated. When did his hair go gray like that, like someone dipped just that tuft in paint?

Overnight? My legs felt wobbly. I held on to the banister; I leaned against it, away from Dad. He seemed to be waiting for me to say something. I headed down the stairs instead, still gripping the banister, moving carefully, taking it slow.

Dad worked frantically around the house, cleaning the bathroom and the kitchen, dusting the living room, putting fresh sheets on the hospital bed, then ripping off those sheets and throwing them into the laundry and putting fresh sheets on their bed upstairs instead. He pushed the hospital bed into the farthest, darkest corner of the living room. When I asked him if I could help, he shook his head wearily and said, "No, get some rest, sweetie. You'll be needing it."

Sweetie? When was the last time Dad called me that?

Now I'm sitting on the roof with a flashlight since there's no moon or stars out tonight. Even the streetlights seem dim. I don't want to lie down in my bed, though I'm tired and I just might sleep when I'm supposed to. But sleeping will bring dreams and tomorrow all the sooner, and Mom, who's barely conscious now, even when she's most awake.

JULY 24

No sleep. No dreams.

We brought Mom home today.

On the way back from the hospital, I sat in the front seat with Dad, and Mom lay stretched out in the back. She looked small on the seat. She looked like she might break. I saw her chart. She weighs seventy-five pounds.

All the way home, Dad talked. He marked our course: "We're turning left, Gracie, hold on. Now here comes a pothole—unavoidable. Big bump. Sorry." He described changes, surprising ones, and the ones Mom would expect, the ones she used to look for to mark seasons passing: "Hey, the Russells' black-eyed Susans are blooming again. Those flowers have taken over their whole yard! And there's Jane Hoover setting up for her garage sale, just like clockwork." Then Dad made promises: "Gayle Foster sent over some new sheets as a homecoming present. You'll like the colors." And: "Trudy Stewart made the chicken broth you love. Tastes as good as ever."

Half of me listened to Dad while the other half thought about the Statue of Liberty puzzle. I finished it right before Dad came to get me today to tell me Mom was ready to come home. Sure enough, some pieces were missing. There was no flame for the statue's torch.

We pulled into our driveway, and Dad turned off the ignition. "Home, sweet home," he said.

Mom didn't make a sound. Her eyes were closed.

Dad twisted around. "Grace?" He lunged over the seat. "Honey?"

I pressed my fists into my stomach, dug my feet into the floorboard, pushed back against my seat. I felt springs give. From deep inside came a dull twang.

"I'm going to Mrs. Ford's." The words exploded from my mouth before I even knew I was saying them. I flung open the car door and bolted, leaving Dad to carry Mom inside the house, like she was no more than a sack of groceries.

I rang the Fords' doorbell three times before Mrs. Ford finally opened it. Her eyes widened when she saw me.

"Livy. What a nice surprise."

"Can I come in?" I asked.

She stepped back, and I slipped inside. I tucked myself into a corner. I wanted to do that—I wanted to make myself smaller, thinner, invisible. Maybe then I wouldn't get in the way. Maybe then I could stay. I bit my lip so hard it hurt.

"Well." Mrs. Ford crossed her arms, then quickly uncrossed them. "The kids are all with their father. It's his day off and he took them to the zoo. So." She looked out the open door behind me, toward our house. Maybe she caught a glimpse of Dad carrying Mom inside. "That's too bad. They would have loved to see you."

"Who?" My voice cracked.

"Why, my kids." Mrs. Ford brushed a coppery strand of hair from her eyes with the back of her hand. Her hand was muddy, and left a streak of dirt on her cheek. "Is there anything I can do?"

I shook my head.

Mrs. Ford shoved her hands into the pockets of her jeans, stared at the floor for a minute, then looked up, her face brightening with an idea. "I'm in the middle of

176

something, but I guess I could use some help."

"I can help," I said.

"You're sure?"

I nodded.

"Actually, you'd be doing me a real favor." Mrs. Ford turned and headed down the hallway. I stayed in the corner for a minute, watching. She bounced when she walked, like she had too much energy and might jump up and touch the ceiling. She walked like a healthy woman. I followed her into the kitchen. I caught up to her there, at the sliding glass door. In the sunlight, I saw that her jeans and clogs were caked with mud.

"I'm gardening," Mrs. Ford said. "But you probably guessed that."

The backyard was torn up. There was a rusted wheelbarrow parked in front of me; it held hunks of grass, and more hunks were stacked nearby. Where the grass had been was black dirt, a big swatch of it, curving along the side of the Fords' yard to their fence. The dirt looked stirred up; Mrs. Ford must have been working it with the muddy hoe that stood propped against the side of the house. A big pile of peat moss spilled across the patio. Next to it were maybe ten plastic buckets holding green, leafy plants, and some wilting, brown sticks that looked like they'd been in the wrong place for way too long. A skinny, little tree lay on the ground, its roots bound up in bulky burlap. Near the tree was a deep hole. But somehow Mrs. Ford's yard looked all right, like that was the way it was supposed to be, on the way to something better.

"Do you know anything about gardening?" Mrs. Ford asked.

Mom always told me what to do, I started to say, but then I shook my head.

"Rats. I was hoping you could teach me." Laughing, Mrs. Ford patted my shoulder. "Don't look so worried. There's nothing to know, really. I have to believe that, or I'd lose all hope." She sighed, looked around the yard. "It's a real mess, isn't it?"

I shook my head again, but she didn't see. She grabbed the hoe, handed it to me. "That bed is almost ready, but I'd love it if you'd go over it once more, find any last clods and break them up. My arms could use a rest."

I set to work. At first, I walked across the dirt carefully, tapping the surface. When nothing much happened, I began to tap harder. Before I knew it, I was hacking away, digging down deep. "Good job," Mrs. Ford said. I didn't look up. Sweat burned my eyes and rolled down my cheeks with tears. I was remembering what it was like to make something beautiful out of a mess, how it felt to garden with Mom.

Finally, I stopped and wiped my arm across my eyes. Mrs. Ford had righted the little tree; she was crouched down beside its root-ball, trying to drag it to the hole. I remembered doing this with Mom once, and how hard it was to lower something that looked so small, but was really so heavy, into that dark, damp place. I remembered how hard it was not to break branches or snap the trunk, and how we struggled to make our tree stand straight. Mom and I planted a redbud tree. Mom loved it; she called it her favorite tree. "If we have to lose our willow," Mom said to me once, "promise me you'll convince Dad to plant a redbud in its place."

Mrs. Ford's tree was a birch. Its white, peeling bark rattled faintly in the wind. As Mrs. Ford pulled, the branches swayed wildly. The birch looked too fragile, like you might peel a few layers away from the trunk and find nothing.

I stuck the hoe into the ground and went to Mrs. Ford. I crouched down beside her. "Just in time," she said. Together we pushed the tree to the edge of the hole. Together we lowered it in. It settled there easily and stood straight.

"Perfect!" Mrs. Ford said.

I grinned at her. But I stopped grinning as quickly as I could. I stopped as quickly as I could, I promise you that. I folded my arms, looked at the ground, and stepped away from Mrs. Ford. I couldn't stand that close to her anymore.

Last year, Dad or Mom or someone asked some church ladies to help me with my Home Ec projects—cooking, sewing, knitting, and other things I hate to do. During my lessons, I couldn't stand too close to those ladies, either. In fact, I could hardly stand to be in the same room with them. They smiled sweet smiles that turned more sour by the hour as those long afternoons wore on, and I burned brownies, it seemed on purpose, and snarled bobbins, it seemed on purpose, and unraveled rows of yarns, it seemed on purpose—or so they must have said to Dad, who always looked at me afterward as if I had something to be sorry about, and asked me repeatedly, "Are you sure you thanked them for all their help?" I wanted those ladies to stop all their help. I didn't like their flowery smells, or their powdered skin, or their helmetlike hairdos; I didn't like their plump bodies pressed warm against mine as they showed me how to darn a sock or knit one, purl two. I didn't like them.

I could feel Mrs. Ford looking at me. She was about

to say something, and I wasn't going to like that, either.

The phone rang. The sound came from deep inside the house, and we might not have heard it if we hadn't, just at that moment, gotten so quiet. We looked at the house and listened as if the sound were supposed to tell us who was calling. We waited through three rings. Finally Mrs. Ford stood, her knees cracking.

"I guess I'd better get that," she said, and went inside.

In a moment, she was back at the door. "It's for you," she called. "Your father."

I followed Mrs. Ford into her kitchen. The phone lay on the countertop, waiting.

Mrs. Ford stood behind me in the doorway. I reached for the phone. My fingers felt thick and stiff, maybe from working in the yard, maybe from the sudden fear I felt. The phone slipped from my hand and clattered against the ceramic. I grabbed it with two hands, held it to my ear.

"Hello?" I said.

I could hear Dad breathing. Other than that, there was silence. I backed myself into the corner between the oven and the refrigerator. I looked out the window above the sink at the yard, at the little tree, sagging now in the wind. Mrs. Ford was going to have to shovel dirt over the roots. She was going to have to stake the trunk to straighten it. She was going to have to mulch the ground. She was going to have to protect the little tree. If she didn't, it would die. I would tell Mrs. Ford all this, I thought, as I waited for Dad to say something. I narrowed my eyes and tried to imagine the birch big and strong, its leaves fluttering proudly in the wind.

When Dad finally spoke, his voice was sharp, like something no one should touch.

"You can't even spend time with your mother on the day she comes home from the hospital. She's over here crying because of you. She *asked* for you. Get home now."

There was a click and a dial tone. He'd hung up on me. I held tightly to the phone. I pressed it hard against my ear. She'd asked for me. I hadn't known she was able to talk anymore.

"I took the library books back this morning," I said.

The dial tone buzzed.

"Oh," I said. "I didn't know you had some to return, too. Okay. I'll be there in a minute. Bye."

I hung up the phone. When I turned around, Mrs. Ford was watching me. She looked quickly away.

"I have to go," I said.

She came over to me. She put her hand lightly on my

shoulders. "You helped so much. Thank you. Come back anytime."

I left Mrs. Ford and ran home. I knew they'd be upstairs. I climbed the stairs slowly and went to their bedroom. Mom lay still on the bed, the new pink sheets smooth over her thin body. Her eyes were closed. Dad stood before the open closet, staring at Mom's clothes. He didn't look at me, but he knew I was home.

"You're too late," he said. He lifted the sleeve of a blue dress and pressed it to his face.

Mom stirred beneath the sheets.

JULY 25

This is a test. This is only a test.
There's nothing human about the voice in my head.

ad was at school getting things organized for football camp; I was keeping watch over Mom. I sat on the love seat in their bedroom. The fan beside the bed stirred up a breeze that lifted the limp curtains and let in a little sunlight. Otherwise the room was in shadows. It was too dim to read, but I had *Gone with the Wind* propped open in my lap.

After an hour or so of our sitting like this, the shaft of sunlight slipped across Mom's face. She opened her eyes and looked at me the way she used to before all this—clearly, steadily.

"Those trees." Her first real words to me in days.

"What?" I said.

"I want to see those trees." Her voice was clear and steady, too.

I stood. *Gone with the Wind* fell with a thud to the floor. "You want to go outside. Out back?"

"No. The cottonwoods. I want to see them."

My ears were ringing. The fan's buzzing suddenly seemed too loud. I switched it off.

"And that little house." Mom tried to push herself up in bed. "I want to see that house, too." She fell back on her pillows, breathing hard.

"You remember the little house?" I asked.

Mom looked at me.

"Dad will be home soon," I began. "Maybe he—"

Mom shook her head. "Dad and I have other things."

"But how will we—"

"We will."

"If you say so." I meant to sound skeptical, but I didn't. I sounded as sure as Mom seemed to feel. I sat down beside her on the bed and drew her arms around my neck. "Hold on," I said. I managed to help her stand. "Hold on," I repeated, my heart thudding. I could drop her; I could hurt her more than she was hurting.

"I'm holding," Mom whispered into my ear.

I half carried her to the bedroom door. There she

settled her arm more comfortably over my shoulder and started, with my help, to walk. It took us some time to make it down the stairs. Mom had to pause and catch her breath after each step. But then we were somehow in the kitchen, somehow at the door.

I caught my breath at a sudden thought. "How will we get there?"

Mom smiled and started to cough. I held her through the spasms. When she'd recovered, she said, "How do you think? The Firebird."

I stared at her. "The Firebird?"

"Got any other suggestions?"

My face went hot. She knew, maybe.

"It's yours," I said.

"Not anymore," Mom said.

"No." Tears stung my eyes.

"All right. It's ours. Think of it like that."

I stared at Mom, astounded. She was herself again. She was going to be okay. She was one of those miracle cases that Pastor Bob is always talking about—what happens when you pray right and often enough, the way God wants. When you pray without ceasing, like the Bible says. Someone must have been praying without ceasing. Dad, maybe, or Pastor Bob or Mrs. Ford. Or maybe God heard me reading Psalm 139 to Mom and took pity on us.

Because there was pink in Mom's cheeks and sparkling clarity in her eyes and speech, and she was a miracle. I believed that today as I helped Mom out the door and into the garage.

She braced herself against the wall while I lifted the garage door. We stood looking at the car for a moment.

"Oh." Mom's hand was at her throat. "I'd forgotten—"

She stopped speaking. My hand was at my throat, too. Mom took a step toward the Firebird and stumbled. I caught her arm, waited until she seemed steady again, then led her to the door on the passenger's side and eased her in. She studied my face as I bent over and lifted her feet, then lowered them onto the floorboard. She knows I've been here, I thought. She can smell me in the seats. She can smell Ed, the faintly sweet smell of antibiotic ointment slathered on his hands.

"You're strong," she said.

"No, I'm not."

"Yes, you are."

"No, I'm not."

Mom sighed and wearily shook her head, but I felt happy. We were bickering. She could still do that.

"I forgot," Mom said. "The keys are in the little box on my dresser."

"Oh," I said, like I didn't know.

When I returned with the keys, Mom was resting her head against the car window. I froze, looking for signs, some new trouble written on her face or body. But her face was peaceful and her body relaxed; her chest rose and fell evenly with each breath. She was asleep, exhausted from her efforts. How long had it been since she'd walked anywhere, since she'd said anything, wanted anything?

I want to see those trees again, she'd said. I could do that for her.

I got into the Firebird and started the engine. I reached across Mom and buckled her seatbelt. I even buckled mine. Then I shifted smoothly into reverse, and backed out of the garage and driveway. I turned onto the street and headed for the cottonwoods, sailing through our sub-division, then onto the road that led out of town and down the hill through the familiar marsh. I slowed as we passed the trailer park and gripped the wheel more tightly, but all I saw were dingy, battered trailers and a tangle of TV antennas, wind chimes, and Christmas lights. I shook my head hard. Why was I thinking about Charlie now? I stole a quick look at Mom. She was resting against the door, her fists tucked under her chin. Her mouth was open and her eyelids fluttered with some dream.

"'For Thou didst form my inward parts.'" I whispered the verse I'd read several times in the past few weeks, hoping Mom would hear it in her sleep. "'Thou didst weave me in my mother's womb. I will give thanks to Thee, for I am fearfully and wonderfully made.'"

We were past the trailer park now. It was only another few miles to Cottonwood Lane. Soon enough, I pulled off the road, next to the field and the trees. I took the key from the ignition and turned to Mom. She was still asleep. Her face was pale again, and the shadows beneath her eyes were almost black.

I unbuckled my seatbelt, then Mom's. Now what? Mom always kept a blanket in the trunk, I remembered. I got out of the car and found it folded neatly beside the spare tire—an old wool blanket that Mom and Dad got just after I was born. My first summers, Mom told me, we used this blanket for picnics and naps. I learned to sit up, crawl, and walk across its green plaid.

Now I slung it over my shoulders like a shawl. It was hot. But I couldn't hold it and Mom. I went to her side of the car and opened her door without thinking. She fell into my arms, limp as a rag doll. I almost dropped her, and that's when she woke, giving a low moan of pain. She stared at me terrified, with no memory, I think, of who I was or where we were.

"We made it," I said.

"Oh," she said softly. "Yes." She wrapped her arms around my neck. Luckily, she was still half sitting on the car seat or I surely would have dropped her. She seemed, in that moment, to expect me to carry her like Dad always does now, like they're just married and he's sweeping her across the threshold. No way was I strong enough to do that. I leaned against the car, letting it support me while I supported Mom.

"You're going to have to walk some," I said.

Mom's face tightened. But then she nodded. I helped her stand, and we started stumbling across the field.

It took us a long time to reach the cottonwoods. By the time we collapsed on the blanket in their deep shade, Mom was crying and I was soaked with sweat. We lay down together on the rough wool. I held Mom's hand, and we didn't say a word. We waited while Mom struggled to breathe. At one point when I didn't think I could stand to hear her anymore—the desperate sounds she made, gulping air—I thought of putting my mouth to hers and trying to help her breathe that way. But I was too afraid to do that, afraid that it wouldn't work, that she would die because I failed. I closed my eyes and tried to pray instead. *Dear God,* I kept praying, *Dear God.* I couldn't get past that.

Finally Mom whispered, "We made it."

"We made it," I shouted to the trees.

Mom closed her eyes for a moment and took a few more ragged breaths. Then she looked at me and smiled. "Listen to the leaves. And look—they're waving to us. Remember? Thousands of hearts saying hello."

"Thousands of hands clapping."

"Blessing," Mom said.

She drifted off to sleep. I looked at her face, trying to memorize it. A fly landed on her cheek. Furious, I waved it away. I leaned over her as if a plague of insects, crows, or vultures might descend out of nowhere and do damage. Mom stirred and groaned, and I put my arm around her. That must have been when I slept.

When I opened my eyes, Mom was watching me. She smiled. "You're still my baby," she said. She pulled me closer and kissed my forehead. She began to rub my back in small, slow circles, and I began to cry because that was the way she used to rub my back, I knew, when I was just born, when she was giving me bottles, and singing me lullabies, and holding me through the night if she had to. There on that old familiar blanket, with Mom's hand on my back rubbing in small, slow circles, I cried. "Hush," Mom whispered. "I'm here."

I lifted my face to hers. "You're getting better, aren't you? I knew you were this morning, and now I really know it. You're getting better, you'll always be here."

"No." Mom looked at me with all her sadness.

I cried myself empty. When I finally stopped, I was thirsty. I hated how thirsty I was, that I had to be bothered with something like that. I pretended I was thinking about Mom.

"Do you need something to drink?" I said. My voice came out in a croak. "Are you hungry?"

She said, "I don't need anything."

"I wish I'd brought a picnic, like we used to."

Mom stared up at the cottonwood leaves. "There's one thing. The little house."

I sat up and looked at the hill that led to the shack that Mom called a house. The hill looked like a mountain. I swallowed hard at the thought of climbing it with Mom.

"We can try," I said.

I helped her stand. But before I could get her arm around my shoulder, her knees buckled and she fell to the blanket again. Her face twisted with pain.

"I'm sorry," she said.

My nails bit into my palms. I couldn't carry her up the hill, that was clear. Could I carry her back to the car? No.

"Mom." I tried to keep my voice steady. I was

remembering Ed, collapsed on the sand, and Gil's suggestion. Gil's suggestion would work now. "I'm going to get the car," I said. "I'll be right back."

Mom stared blankly at the shifting cottonwood leaves. She wouldn't look at me. She was concentrating on breathing. I turned and ran toward the car, grass whipping against my legs. I kept my eyes on the ground, looking for holes or stones, anything that might make me trip or fall. I couldn't do anything more stupid than I'd already done by bringing Mom here; I couldn't make things worse.

Finally at the car, I threw myself inside and drove into the field. I was sure Mom was dead when I saw her still, white form on the blanket. But then, through the open window, I heard her moaning. Somehow I lifted her into the backseat, and tucked up her legs. She curled into herself.

I drove straight home, faster than I've ever driven before, faster than I've ever been driven.

Dad was standing in the empty garage, waiting for me. I wanted him to yell at me or slap me, but he didn't. He held me tightly. He let go almost before I'd realized that I was in his arms. Without saying a word, he got in the car and drove away with Mom.

Inside the house, every light was on and the TV was

going. Olympic swimmers crawled through neon blue, just to touch a wall. I went upstairs to Mom and Dad's bedroom. There was a sunken place in the mattress where she lay just this morning. I looked at that sunken place until I could almost see her there and hear her voice, asking me to take her to those trees. I lay down on the bed and breathed in her scent—the smell of her body dying, a smell I used to hate.

I lay there until the TV picture downstairs changed to a test pattern. I knew this had happened because I could hear a faint voice—a voice that was supposed to reassure me, but didn't because there was nothing human about it, the human was gone. It was the cold voice of a machine saying over and over again, *This is a test. This isn't an emergency. This is only a test.* I didn't believe it for a minute.

Mom and I stand beneath the cottonwoods. She holds my hand in hers; she's got the grip of a strong, healthy woman. I am the age I am now, yet I want her to pick me up and hold me. I move closer to her. She looks at me, and though I don't say a word, she nods. She bends slightly, ready to cradle me in her arms. She is strong enough to do this; she will not falter or collapse. I lean into her and relax.

The leaves above us rustle as if stirred by wind, though there is no wind; the air is as calm and steady as our breathing. In the next moment, the branches are storm-tossed against a cloudless blue sky. The branches pitch and heave, wood creaking, snapping. Below us, the tangled roots groan as their hold on the earth loosens. Mom cries out. We stagger away from the trees, but too late—heavy, splintered limbs fall around us. Massive trunks sway and thunder down; twisted roots jut toward the sky. In the silence that follows, I look for Mom, but I can't find her. I am alone, imprisoned in a tangle of trees.

*T*his room they shared will be only his. This window. This mirror. This bed. And me.

JULY 27 (nearly dawn)

*D*ad finally came for me last night, in the middle of the night. He woke me from their bed, where I had been sleeping off and on through yesterday and into last night. "Come on," was all he said. He drove me to the hospital, took me up some stairs, led me down a bright, empty hall, and through a door to Mom. She lifted her hand and I took it, but before either of us could say a word, her hand slipped from mine and she closed her eyes. Dad turned and left the room. I knew I was to follow him, and I did, thinking: this is just a dream.

JULY 27 (nearly night)

You've got it pretty good, if you bother to remember your dreams. If your mind still works like that.

This morning, I found Dad sitting on their bed, holding Mom's pillow. When I came into the room, he raised his head. His face was horrible to look at. I wanted to run; I was going to run. But Dad started to cry. He bowed beneath the force of his sobs. He seemed far away, like the room had expanded and he was a stranger on the other side. I could have stood there forever, watching him across such a great distance, if it hadn't been for the sounds he was making. When someone makes sounds like that, you can't stop yourself from moving closer. I sat down on the edge of the bed. I put my hand on his arm, and he clutched my hand. He didn't stop crying. I began patting Dad's arm, saying, "It's all right. Don't cry. Please don't cry. Please stop crying. Please. Stop crying now."

He didn't stop. I got up and took hold of his shoulders. I felt like my hands on his shoulders were the things holding him together; if I took my hands away, he'd break into pieces like a clay statue. And I could barely hold him together—not with the way the room was expanding and contracting with his sobs. The room was going to collapse because he was going to collapse. Everything was going to collapse. He had to stop crying.

So I shook him. I shook him as hard as I could.

"Dad. Stop crying." I was screaming. "Stop it now. Stop."

He stopped. The room went quiet so quickly, it seemed like he'd never cried at all, though his face and neck were wet, and down the front of his blue shirt were the dark stains of tears.

"She's gone," Dad said dully.

"I know that." I sounded irritated, almost bored.

"I bought a plot yesterday." Dad pulled the pillow to his chest and hunched over it. "That's where I was. I should have been with her all day. But I was out shopping for her grave, and she died without me."

"A plot?" I couldn't think what that was.

"You took her out to see those cottonwoods." He looked at me, but there was no anger in his look, no accusation. He seemed hungry for something that I might be able to give him. "What happened? What did she say?"

"A plot?" My thoughts felt like dumb and fumbling hands, trying to grab hold of that word and catch the shape of its meaning. I thought of a conspiracy. I thought of what we had learned in English class: rising action, climax, falling action—the inverted check mark that our teacher kept scratching across the blackboard all last spring.

Dad closed his eyes tightly for a moment. "A nice plot at the Troy City Cemetery. Under a yew tree. The nicest one they had." His mouth twisted. "Please. What happened?"

I could smell her in the sheets. This is how her ghost will smell, I thought. I sat very still and stared at the bed where her body had been. He wants me to say that I hurt her worse than she was hurting, I thought. He wants me to say that I caused her death. He wants me to tell him I'm sorry for what I did, so he doesn't have to feel sorry for what he didn't do.

"Did she ask for me?" Dad asked.

I looked at him. Still no anger, no accusation. "She slept most of the time we were there."

"Nothing happened?"

"Nothing much." I held myself tight. I was lying.

"She said it was wonderful, going there with you." Dad put his hand on my shoulder. "She said it meant everything."

He gave those words to me, like a gift, then he took his hand away.

JULY 29

Everything is a nightmare.

*H*e found me in the kitchen. "Come on," he said. He took me up to their room. I stopped in the doorway at the sight of Mom's stuff dumped out on the bed and the floor. Her drawers empty and open. Her side of the closet bare. Boxes and garbage bags heaped on the love seat. Dad went to the bed. He picked up one of Mom's scarves, then one of her blouses. He looked at these things like they were mysteries, things he'd never seen before, that were possibly dangerous.

"I'm going through her—" he paused, staring at Mom's blouse. "I'm trying to decide what we should donate to Goodwill, what her friends might use, what you might want to keep." He dropped the scarf and blouse back on the bed. "I can't."

He left the room. I ran after him, down the hallway to the top of the stairs. He was already near the bottom.

"I was making a sandwich," I said.

He looked at me. "Start by putting things into piles. Goodwill. Friends. You. It's all got to be out of here by tomorrow, at the latest."

"Wait." My voice squeaked high, a yelp. "Why so soon?"

"Soon?" His hands slammed down on the banister. "It's not soon enough!" He looked at me, and his face softened. "Livy. It's gotta go. It might as well be now. And, listen, they want an outfit for her at the funeral home. Pick something out, something pretty. You'll be better at that than me."

Mom's stuff was marked. Some of it, anyway. A lipstick smudge. A coffee spill, an ink spot, a perfume stain. Everything held the shape and smell of her body. I lifted up an old nylon and saw the way her foot once filled it. And there was her favorite sweater—the one with the holes where her elbows rubbed. And her most comfortable corduroy pants, with the knees worn thin and shiny. These were the clothes Mom always said she had to get rid of, but never did; these were the clothes I didn't want to see, any more than Dad did. They felt like they might explode in my hands, charged with too many memories.

In the end, these were the clothes that I ended up keeping for myself, along with almost everything else. I packed five boxes for me, one box for Goodwill (of things she never liked and I never saw her touch), and one box for friends. This last was the hardest part. Some of the stuff I wanted to keep. But then I remembered a friend who said she loved a particular pair of gloves, and another friend who gave a sparkly pin to Mom and always commented when Mom wore it, and someone else who could fit into the coat that was already too narrow for my shoulders. In this way, I worked through a list of Mom's friends and acquaintances, trying to pretend that I was distributing her things the way I might distribute a deck of cards: I could always call a misdeal and collect everything again.

I didn't let myself think too long about an outfit for the funeral home. I grabbed a lavender silk shirt she'd always liked—one Dad gave her for their anniversary a few years ago—and a long black velvet skirt that I'd always loved, because she only wore it for holidays or special occasions, and when she wore it she looked beautiful and happy. I folded this outfit and put it into a paper bag. Then I dug through her jewelry until I found the box that held the heart-shaped necklace with the amethyst chip that I gave her two years ago for her birthday. I'd saved and saved for the necklace, and still had to borrow money from Dad, but at the time I thought it worth every penny. Plus, I was sure no one but me had bothered to figure out what Mom's birthstone was—let alone her zodiac sign and horoscope, which was printed on the inside of the box. I opened the box, nudged the pendant aside, and read the inscription: AQUARIUS, WATER BEARER. FLUID BY NATURE, YOU LIKE TO GO WITH THE FLOW. YOU HAVE THE ABILITY TO TRANSFORM YOURSELF, AND SEEK MANY DIFFERENT EMOTIONAL AND PHYSICAL STATES. I snapped the box shut and put the necklace into the bag with her outfit.

Then I knelt down by her lingerie. I'd saved this pile for last. The soft, cotton garments might as well have been warm from her skin, her perfume lingered so richly there. Roses. I selected a bra, panties, slip, and pair of hose, put these things into the paper bag with the outfit. Then I sat down again by the pile. My hands moved over nightgown after nightgown. In this one she rocked me to sleep. In this one she held me when I was sick. In this one she soothed my bad dreams.

At the bottom of the pile, I discovered my favorite of her gowns—the one she always wore on Christmas morning. I recognized it before I even saw its red fabric, my fingers registering the soft worn flannel, the tiny pearl buttons. I lifted it and hugged it close, then drew in a breath. The gown was rolled into a ball; there was something hard and bulky at its center. I held the gown out. Slowly, I let it unfold.

Inside were five small books tied together with a black ribbon. I carefully untied the ribbon; one by one, I studied the books. Each was bound in smooth red leather; each cover was embossed in gold with a date. 1990 marked the first book. Then came '91, '92, '93, and '94.

I opened up 1990. There was Mom's handwriting, filling the first page. I flipped through the other pages, to see her handwriting again and again—her letters perfectly penciled, inscribed with precision and care. I'd discovered Mom's journals, hidden among her most private things, buried in a place she must have assumed no one would look. For a moment, I knelt on the floor, barely able to catch my breath, her journals spread before me. Then, quickly, clumsily, I got up and stuffed her jewelry case and her lingerie into one of my five boxes. I gathered up her journals—each no longer than my hand. Then I ran to my room and closed the door. I sat down on my bed and opened up 1990—the year I was born. The first entry was dated the day before my birth:

August 21, 1990
The day started out routine.
At 5:00 I prepared supper.
I did not feel well so at 9:30 I went to bed.
At 11:30 I awoke and went to the bathroom.
My water broke. Warden took me to the hospital.
We arrived at the hospital at 1:00 a.m.

Here's what she wrote on the day I was born, August 22, 1990:

Olivia was born today. Olivia Moore.
A little girl.
I wanted a natural birth, but they had to give me drugs.
I begged for drugs.
Our bill was minimal.
Blue Cross paid most of it.
It's the phone calls that get you every time.

I read the rest of August, September, and October; I read the rest of 1990. I read these entries twice to make sure, but all of them are like my birthday—the facts and nothing but the facts, written neatly, each line a statement, so that it seems like Mom turned the day into a list. She pressed so lightly with her pencil that sometimes I could barely read the words; a few times, I couldn't. And then there are the words she scratched out and the words she tried to erase, leaving smudges, sometimes rubbing through the paper altogether.

There's nothing about what Mom *felt*. Nothing. Maybe she felt nothing. I'll never really know now, will I? I closed Mom's journal and stuffed it under my mattress. I didn't care what she cooked for supper in 1990, how many diapers I'd soiled, what neighbor came to visit, if it rained. I looked through 1991, 1992, and 1993 and they were the same. I stuffed them under my mattress with 1990. I picked up 1994, and, without even opening it, I hid it there, too, pushing hard enough to bend back the pages. Goodwill wouldn't want Mom's journals. Her friends wouldn't want them either. If I had the energy, I'd throw them in the garbage.

What I know now is this: in the back of my mind, writing this journal, I've been writing to Mom. I've been filling these pages up for you, Mom, telling you all the stuff I do, and also all the stuff I've been thinking and feeling—all the stuff you've been missing. You've been here in every letter, syllable, word, sentence, paragraph, page, entry. I've been filling you in, fleshing stuff out, giving you all that I can. Writing and writing, because somewhere deep inside, I believed that if I revealed enough, you'd go looking for my secrets someday. You'd scrounge through my room the way normal mothers do, searching for sex manuals and rubbers, cigarettes and bongs—searching for this journal. You'd discover it hidden in my desk drawer; you'd steal it away like I stole yours. You'd open it and read, feel angry and betrayed. We'd have a knock-down-drag-out fight. You'd yell at me, ground me; you'd really let me have it. In ten years, twenty years, thirty years, we'd laugh about everything. You'd live that long.

AUGUST 1

Mrs. Ford gave me a pill, and the night went black.

*W*hen I walked into the Troy City Funeral Home today, and saw Mom lying in a coffin in her lavender blouse and black velvet skirt, I closed my eyes. I stood in the middle of the visitation parlor with my eyes closed until someone slipped their arm through mine and steadied me.

"She looks beautiful. She does."

I opened my eyes. Ruth was standing beside me, holding me tight, telling me lies. I knew from across the room that Mom did not look beautiful. She wasn't beautiful anymore.

"Thanks," I said to Ruth, but not for the compliment, for being there.

"You're welcome," she said.

Ruth steered me across the room to the couch where I sat all day, through all kinds of visitors, including Ruth's parents, who had all the right lines for an occasion such as this. Ruth didn't leave when they did; she stayed beside me, as one by one, kids from school showed up and had no idea what to say. Most of them didn't do much more than look at me warily, like I might be contagious. They didn't get too close. Quietly, cautiously, they would go over to Dad and shake his hand.

Gil, Jackie, and Ed were the exceptions. Gil and Jackie pulled up chairs and sat with Ruth and me. Gil made some jokes. I can't remember what they were, but I do remember laughing—a sound like glass breaking. Jackie said she would call me in a few days, and I knew she meant it. Then Ed poked his head in and waved. His bandages looked less bulky. It looked like it was easier for him to do simple things like wave. I wanted to tell him that. But I couldn't imagine speaking loudly enough to be heard across the parlor. And besides, he'd already left.

"Don't worry," Jackie said, catching my eye.

Gil nodded. "If I know Ed, he'll be back."

And he was. Ed came back right away, carrying a

cardboard drink tray with root beer floats for Ruth, Jackie, Gil, and me. I thanked him, though the sweet smell alone made me feel sick. Ruth drank hers and then mine, and when I laughed at her little mustache of foam, she didn't lick it away.

Then one by one they had to hug me and leave. And I was mostly alone on the couch.

In the evening, Mrs. Ford came, carrying a vase filled with flowers from her garden. She set her flowers off to one side of Mom's casket. They looked small and plain next to all the other lavish arrangements. Most people probably didn't even notice them, but I thought they were the loveliest flowers there. I watched Mrs. Ford work to stop crying. She stood quietly in the corner with her head bowed. Then she took a deep breath, crossed the room, and held me. She didn't speak; she didn't seem to expect me to speak, either. She held me until I had to pull away.

It was dark by then. Mrs. Ford was one of the last ones to leave. I was still sitting on the couch, staring at the floor, when all of a sudden, there were Dad's black shoes toe to toe with mine. We'd hardly spoken all day. Once, he'd asked me if I was hungry. Another time, he'd handed me a glass of water.

"Well," he said now. "That's over."

I nodded, and when I did that Dad started to laugh, silently at first, then "Ha, Ha, Ha," until he had tears in his eyes. "Thank God," Dad managed to say. He put his hand to his mouth to hide his laughter. When he lowered his hand a moment later, he wasn't laughing anymore. His mouth was set in a firm line. I felt better, safer, seeing him back to his familiar self—the self that didn't cry or laugh. Dad rocked back and forth on his heels. He reached out and gave my arm a quick shake. "Say goodbye now, Livy," he said, then he turned and walked out of the room.

I stayed on the couch, my hands folded in my lap. I looked at my hands. Unfolded them. Folded them again.

"Bye," I said as softly as I could, and jumped up, startled by the sound of my voice so loud in the silent room. I tested my legs; they felt wobbly but they worked. I was walking. I was standing in front of the casket.

"Mom?" I said.

She lay there in a bed of white satin, a lacy pillow beneath her head. Her hands were crossed over her chest, her fingers pressed together, stiff and perfectly straight, like they'd been glued into place. Her mouth looked that way too. Someone had spread lipstick on her lips, and there was a thick line of it where her lips met, as if to cover whatever held them closed. The color was bright pink, a

213

shade she never wore, and her eyelids were powdered blue. There were circles of blush on her sharp cheekbones, and thick tan makeup on the sunken skin beneath that— makeup that spread all over her face and down her neck to her chest, where the lavender blouse opened. The little silver necklace looked all wrong—that heart against a tan throat that should have been pale and freckled. But her hair was maybe the strangest thing of all. Someone had styled it, given it shine and fullness, then stiffened it with hair spray—but they had styled it the way Mom styled her hair five years ago. And her hair was brown again, not at all gray. It was like someone had seen an old picture of Mom, one from when she was happy and healthy, when cancer was something other people got. Someone had tried to make her look like that again.

"I'm sorry," I said. She didn't stir. "I didn't mean to," I said. "I'm sorry."

Sorry that I left her when she came home from the hospital, and ran away to Mrs. Ford's. Sorry for all those times I stayed in my room and read *Gone with the Wind*, when I should have been keeping her company instead. Sorry for reading her journals, and then being disappointed and angry because they weren't what I wanted them to be. Sorry for taking her to the cottonwoods, for hastening her death.

I shut my eyes, tried to make myself cry. I opened my eyes, and I wasn't crying.

"Livy." Dad's voice came from behind me.

I looked at Mom lying there, already so far away, already someone I could hardly remember. I looked and looked at her, then I looked at Dad. We stood there for a moment, Dad and me, showing each other nothing but blank faces. When you show someone a face like that for long enough, you feel blank inside, too. So I didn't feel anything, walking past Dad. I didn't feel anything when he touched my arm and held on for a moment; I didn't feel anything when I pulled away and kept walking, right out of the funeral home. I didn't feel anything, but I knew that I wanted to be far away when Dad said good-bye to Mom, when he closed the lid on the casket and left her in darkness.

AUGUST 2

Another pill. Another night of nothing.

"This is a celebration," Pastor Bob said at the funeral. "Grace has gone on to a better place."

There were flowers and music. The casket was closed. It almost looked like a celebration.

I didn't cry. Dad did, hard, at the very end, as we stood and followed the casket from the church.

Then came the slow, silent car ride to the cemetery, and the slow, silent walk to the grave. Then the hole under her casket. Someone pushed a white lily into my hand, and I dropped it down onto the glossy wood. Mom never liked lilies. They reminded her of death, she said.

We came back to a house full of people dressed in black, who kept bringing me glass plates piled with food and glass cups filled with red punch.

Finally the people are gone. The kitchen is clean, no sign that anyone was ever here, except for the food sealed in Tupperware, spread across the counters, stacked in the fridge, stuffed into the freezer, waiting to rot.

℘rs. Ford stopped giving me pills, but that's okay, because I have no problem sleeping now. I sleep a lot. I've given up on dreams for good, I guess. Or maybe they've given up on me. I don't even bother going out on the roof anymore. Once in a blue moon I eat; I take a bath.

The moonlight is like a cool sheet, the sunlight like an electric blanket, the shadow like her shadow against my wall. I can change the look of things just by closing my eyes.

I wake up to notes from Dad taped to my pillow: RUTH CALLED. JACKIE CALLED. ED CALLED, AGAIN. I let these notes drift to the floor. I close my eyes.

Then today I saw something silver glinting on my desk. Keys. Like I need another set of keys, I thought, meaning: to this empty house. Then I made it out of bed and picked up the keys and realized what they unlocked.

I guess I don't have to ask Dad's permission. He gave me his permission by giving me the keys. She gave me her permission, too, but I still want to ask her.

How do I do that?

Do I look up at the sky and say, Please? I know you said it's all right, but is it really all right?

Is it all right if I borrow your car?

AUGUST 12

*N*ot much smells like her now, since Dad put my boxes filled with her things somewhere in the basement and then washed the sheets where she once slept.

Except the Firebird.

I took it out for the first time today. I made it to the end of the street, but then I had to pull over. I couldn't go any farther. I sat in the car. The smell of her perfume was strongest on the steering wheel, where she used to rest her wrists. Roses.

It was almost too hot to breathe with the convertible top up and the air-conditioning off. But I didn't open the windows. Things escape too easily into thin air.

AUGUST 16

I'm dreaming again, of ashy roses and steely thorns and lilies she never liked, rotting on their stalks.

There are so many roads I never knew about. I've emptied almost two whole tanks—not thinking, just driving. Sometimes I stop the car. I don't get out. I sit inside and stare at whatever. Like right now. I'm staring at our garage wall—at her red bike that hangs upside down, suspended from the ceiling by its tires. Once, she biked with me to the little shack off Cottonwood Lane. "Never again," she kept panting the whole way home.

She was right.

The one road I never drive down now is Cottonwood Lane.

Today, passing the high school, I spotted Dad. He

was walking toward the gym, his head and shoulders bowed, his hands in his pockets; he was walking like an old man, moving his feet like they were made of lead, slowly making his way.

He stopped and lifted his head, the way I've seen dogs do when they smell something familiar or strange. I gripped the steering wheel as Dad looked right at the Firebird. We've barely seen each other these last weeks, and he's never been around to see me pull the car out of the driveway or return it to the garage. Dad's eyes widened at the sight of me behind the wheel; he came to attention and stood up straight. He raised his hand and waved.

I waved back. Then I pressed the accelerator to the floor and drove away.

Much later, I drove past the cemetery. I wasn't thinking. It was dark, and the gravestones flickered in the moonlight, trying to get my attention. I ducked my head, almost drove off the road. I won't go that way again, either.

AUGUST 19

Gravestones, flickering in the moonlight, trying to get my attention.

That was it—enough to awaken me. It was barely daybreak, but I got dressed. I found my purse and gave it a good shake, listening for the car keys. The clutter inside bumped around, but there was no reassuring jangle.

I had to get out of the house, away from my dream. I dumped the purse upside down and sorted through the small pile, but the keys weren't there. I was sweating now.

I took a step back and my foot came down on something sharp. It bit into my heel, but I let out a sigh, relieved. The keys had fallen to the floor. I bent to pick them up, and that's when I caught sight of something poking out from under my mattress. I tugged at it, and pulled out the last of Mom's journals. 1994.

I held the journal out from me, the way I might hold a cat that scratches. Mom touched this, I thought. I tried to remember her hands, touching things, but that was too easy—I only had to look at my own hands. So I tried to remember the sound of Mom's voice, her laugh, but all I could hear was silence, thick and pressing in where words and laughter should be. I tried to remember the way she walked, but all I could see were empty shoes—the plain, brown pumps that she loved, that would always be too narrow for me to wear. I tried to remember her face, but all I could see was something like a blurry photograph, that might have been a picture of any woman.

The silence pressed in harder.

I sat down on my bed and opened her journal. The pages were empty. All of them. I leafed through it, and every line was blank. Nothing happened in 1994; nothing even worthy of a list.

I threw the journal into the wastebasket. It landed with a dull thud. I got up, grabbed the car keys, and headed out my door. I was almost at the bottom of the stairs, when I turned around and went back to my room. I lifted Mom's journal from the garbage. Somewhere, at some time, she had touched it. I pressed it to my chest. Then I opened it again.

This time I noticed that the first page was slightly dog-eared. In her other journals, Mom hadn't written on the very first page; she's always left it blank—as if the first page were some kind of special introductory section, the place where a dedication would be made, when everything had been written and understood. I turned to this page and found Mom's letter.

> *July 1*
> *Dear Livy,*
> *I guess I don't have to tell you that I'm dying. Somehow you've learned this since yesterday. I see the change in you—your sweet eyes, stunned and dulled.*
> *What I want to tell you is that my love won't die. I will love you, even after I'm gone. My love is that strong.*
> *Don't be scared.*
> *Never give up. Mom*

I reread my journal entry from July 1. On that day, Dad left the house, and I took care of Mom. I told her that I was keeping a journal—the journal she gave to me. What I didn't know was this: On July 1, some time after our talk, Mom climbed the stairs, dug through her drawer, found her old journals, and wrote this letter to me. Somehow she bound the journals with a ribbon and hid them again, then returned to the living room and got back into the hospital bed. She cared enough about me to do all this with the little life she had left inside.

I guess she believed in her words enough to know that they'd reach me somehow—what she couldn't say out loud.

I read the letter until the sentences blurred together, and the last line became *Never give up Mom.* I knew then that I'd never give her up; I'd find a way to be her daughter even now that she was dead.

Please remember me.

That's what a dying person might write, you'd think so anyway. *I've vanished, please don't forget me, please remember.* But Mom didn't write that. She wrote: *Don't be scared.* And: *Never give up.*

Get on with your life, she might have added, if she'd had the strength and time. *You can do anything.*

AUGUST 25

I open Mom's journal and it's filled with letters
from her, all of them to me, all of them telling me
things she always wanted to say.

Not blank after all.

I woke up crying this morning, knowing the pages
were still empty; even she can't work that kind of magic.
From outside came a shrill whine I couldn't have slept
through anyway. I jumped from my bed and went to the
window.

Dad was cutting down the blighted willow.

Apparently, he'd borrowed Sheriff Byrne's chain saw,
because Sheriff Byrne stood beside him, giving direc-
tions, pointing at the tree's trunk, showing Dad where to

place the saw's long, fierce-looking blade, where to let 'er rip. Chips of wood spewed into the air and showered down on Dad, clung to his hair, his clothes.

Dad wasn't wearing goggles. I brushed the tears from my eyes. He's all I've got, I thought.

I ran downstairs, grabbed Dad's sunglasses from the kitchen counter, and sprinted outside.

Dad and Sheriff Byrne had their backs to me.

"Hey!" I yelled. "Stop!"

They didn't hear me, they didn't turn around.

Then a wood chip hit Dad below his eye, on his cheek. He dropped the saw and clapped his hands over his face. I screamed as the blade chewed grass right at Dad's feet. Then the saw went dead. Dad flicked a splinter of wood from his face. He turned toward me, dazed.

"Here," I said, and held out the sunglasses.

Dad nodded obediently and took the sunglasses. A soft breeze stirred, and the willow rocked on its ravaged trunk.

Sheriff Byrne said, "Stand back from the tree a bit, Ward."

"It had to come down," Dad said to me. His voice was gruff—responding to some accusation I hadn't made. "You know it had to come down. She kept putting it off. It's a giant weed."

228

For the first time, I heard Mom's quiet firm voice again, loud and clear: "Don't say that. It's a beautiful tree, Warden."

Dad took a step toward me. "Excuse me?"

I swallowed hard. That had been me talking, not Mom. I put my hand to my throat.

"Ward." Sheriff Byrne stepped between us. "It's not too late to get help. We can call some of your jocks. They'll be glad to lend a hand with this thing."

Dad said, "I don't need anyone's help."

"Oh, yes you do." Mrs. Ford had come up behind us, quiet as a deer. She was wearing her gardening clothes—her worn jeans and sweat-stained shirt, her stiff, mud-caked gloves and straw hat. "You definitely need help with that, Ward." Mrs. Ford peered past me at the willow tree, her eyes narrowed. "I don't know much about willows, but I know that."

"At least wear your sunglasses," I said.

"Livy." Dad pointed at the house. "Go inside."

I didn't move.

Dad put on the sunglasses and grabbed the chain saw. His turned his back on us, but he couldn't hide the fact that his shoulders were shaking.

Sheriff Byrne peered at him. "Ward?"

Mrs. Ford put her arm around me.

Dad waved a hand at us, but he didn't turn around. "I'm busy, can't you see that?" His voice was muffled. "I can't talk right now."

"Well then," Mrs. Ford said, "do you mind if I borrow Livy?"

Dad gave a quick shrug. "Sure, borrow her." Keep her, it sounded like.

"Come on, Livy," Mrs. Ford said briskly. "We've got work to do, too."

She really didn't need my help, I knew that. She was puttering, mostly, putting in a few small bushes. She'd gotten them at an end-of-the-season sale, she said, and she wanted to plant them now so their roots had time to settle. "You can plant something too late," she said, "and it'll freeze, poor thing. It won't have a chance if it doesn't have the right protection."

We were working side by side, with just one more bush to go, when Mrs. Ford suddenly pulled me to my feet and walked me over to a small tree, still bound in its root-ball.

"I want to give you this," she said, fingering the tree's branches. "If your dad manages to get the willow out, you could plant this redbud in its spot. Your mom would have wanted something there. She once told me that she loved redbuds."

I touched one of the spindly branches. "Thank you," I said. For everything, I didn't say.

Around lunchtime, I pushed the redbud home in Mrs. Ford's wheelbarrow. Sheriff Byrne was gone, and so was his chain saw, but Dad was still in the backyard, digging away at the willow's stump, trying to uproot it. The rest of the willow now lay in pieces beside the fence.

I watered the redbud and left it in the shade of the garage. Even now, sitting at the kitchen table, eating leftovers I can't taste, I can still hear Dad chopping away at the hard, dry earth with his shovel. I can hear his voice, too, the way it rises and falls, calling for Grace.

AUGUST 26

One summer afternoon, we worked in the garden, planting roses near the willow tree, weeding until sweat dripped into our eyes, drinking iced tea straight from the pitcher because glasses didn't seem big enough.

It all came back to me in a dream.

*D*ad gave up digging after dark last night. He threw the shovel to the ground, stormed into the house and up the stairs. He slammed into the bathroom. The shower came on full blast.

I was holding *Gone with the Wind* again, making myself read the part I'd been skipping all summer—the part where Scarlett comes home and finds her mother dead. It was hard, but I was doing it. I'd decided to get through that section, then put the book away for good.

Then a rock hit my window, rattling the screen.

I edged my way off the bed and peered through the slats of the blind. Ed stood on the cement patio below. He waved at me from under the back porch light. He cupped his bandaged hands around his mouth and spoke in a stage whisper. "Come down. I'll be out front." He raised his voice a bit. "No excuses." Then he was gone, slipping into the shadows.

I needed some time to think, so I found a place for *Gone with the Wind* on my bookshelf. As I pushed the book into place, I remembered what Mom had written in her journal. "Never give up," I said aloud, in case she was listening. I pulled on a pair of sandals and grabbed the car keys from my desk. The bathroom was right across the hall from my room. I went and leaned up against the closed door. On the other side, the shower streamed.

"I'm going out," I yelled.

The shower stopped. After a few moments, Dad cracked the door. He peered at me through wisps of steam.

"You're grounded," he said.

"You've got to be kidding."

"No."

"Give me a break."

"I've been giving you a break."

"Oh, yeah?"

"Yeah." He glared at me. "You know what I told you."

"You told me to take care of myself. So that's what I've been doing. For months."

"I told you—" Something like fear flitted across Dad's face. "Months?" He cleared his throat. "God help me. It doesn't matter anymore, anyway. But I want you to remember one thing, Livy. One thing. Boys sow wild oats and girls become tramps."

"Great. Now I can really take care of myself." I turned away before Dad could shut the door in my face. Then I ran downstairs and out of the house.

Ed was standing beside the garage. He gingerly rubbed his wrists together, like the skin there itched beneath the gauze. "Can you drive?"

"Yeah." I couldn't help but smile at the question. "I've been getting a lot of practice. Did you walk here?"

"I got tired of waiting around for you to call me back. It's not that far. My feet still work fine."

But it wasn't close, I knew that. Ed had covered a couple of miles to get to my house.

"Come on," I said. I opened the garage door, and we got inside the Firebird. "Where to?" I said when we were safely out of the driveway. In the rearview mirror there was still no sight of Dad waving me back to take my punishment.

"Where else?" Ed tried to roll down his window and couldn't. Roses, I thought. But then I reached across him and rolled it down myself. Ed smiled his thanks and said, "Chloe's."

"Great." I locked my gaze on the road. "What's the occasion?"

"Gil."

"Gil's an occasion?"

"Chloe's no dummy. She caters to cool people even when she hates them. Gil's leaving tomorrow, and so she's hosting a little send-off."

"Wow." I braked at a red light. "I feel honored to be included."

As we waited for the light to change, I took a long look at Ed. His hair was wet and smelled clean, and he wore a crisp yellow shirt. Now that the window was all the way down, he'd draped his arm over the door. When the light turned green and we drove on, Ed held out his hand; it looked like he was trying to air out his bandages. His hand rode the air currents like a bird. Ed smiled.

"Doesn't that hurt," I said, "the wind like that?"

"A little." Ed shrugged. "It's worth it, though."

We didn't say anything for a while as we drove deeper into the country. Ed whistled a little tune through his teeth as we made the turn for Chloe's place. A long line of cars snaked down the long driveway and up the road. I parked at the end of it, my heart thudding in my chest. I felt like I'd never left my house in my life.

Ed cleared his throat. "I could use a little help opening my door."

That's what got me out of the Firebird. Now I'm helping boys *out* of cars, too, I thought, and then: I can't wait to tell Ruth.

I asked Ed if she'd be at the party, but he didn't know. All the way up the driveway, he kept making jokes—the kind of forgettable puns grade school kids tell when they're feeling particularly silly. Before I knew it, I was giddy with laughter, and we were standing at the entrance to Chloe's barn.

Turned out, this was more than a little send-off. Chloe had turned the barn into a regular dance club, and she hadn't held back on the guest list, either. Herds of people were there—and not just sophomores—dancing, eating, drinking.

I hesitated for a moment, but Ed cautiously put his arm around my shoulder and guided me through the crowd to the food table. We'd just loaded up our plates when Chloe appeared before us wearing a pair of pale pink shorts and a white camisole. Of course, I hadn't been able to dress for the occasion. I was wearing an old pair of cutoffs and a striped cotton shirt—one I first wore in eighth grade, with a frayed collar and a missing button just above my waist. Chloe gave me a quick once-over and frowned.

"Hi." She turned to Ed. "Looks like you're feeling better."

"Looks like it." Ed raised his eyebrows as the music got even louder. "Your parents must be out of town. Or else they're deep sleepers."

"My mother and my *step*father are in Italy," Chloe said flatly. "My little brother and his *au pair* are deep sleepers." Chloe turned to me. "I wanted to tell you, Livy, that your mother's funeral was really moving. And you were amazing, the way you stayed so calm. I never could have done that. I would have lost it if my mother had died."

I couldn't say anything. I just looked at her.

Ed said, "You always think of the sweetest things to say, Chloe. Really."

Chloe looked quickly at the dusty floor. When she looked up again, her eyes were brimming with tears.

"I'm sorry." Chloe's voice could hardly be heard over

the music. "I'm so sorry." She leaned into me. "I didn't mean to be stupid. I just don't know what to say. I *don't* know what I'd do if my mom died. I keep thinking about you and—"

"It's okay." I put my hand on her arm, more to keep her from coming closer to me than to reassure her. "I don't know what to say either."

"I mean, how do you handle it?"

"I don't know."

Chloe's breath smelled thickly sweet. I felt a wave of sickness, and remembered: Boone's Farm. I took a step back. "Am I handling it?"

Chloe shrugged sadly. Then some guy pulled her away to dance. Soon she was laughing in his arms.

"There she goes." Gil came up to Ed and me. He rolled his eyes. "Obviously, she can't get along without me."

Ed laughed. "Obviously."

"Chloe's all right." I gestured to the table of food, the speakers booming music. "She's definitely generous."

But something in my chest felt heavy. I wasn't "handling it" at all. I shouldn't have come to this party. I could barely bring myself to look anyone in the eye—these kids I once knew who now felt like strangers.

I grabbed a beer, opened it, took a long swig. Ed was

watching me closely, so I looked out at the dancers. Gil was in the thick of things again, prowling through the crowd, brushing up against girls, laughing with guys. Jackie was there, too, dancing on her own, lost in the music. Jackie didn't care what anybody thought. She was the kind of girl Mom hoped I would be, a girl who never got scared, who never gave up.

Jackie must have felt me thinking about her, because she looked right at me then. She smiled wryly—*We both know what's what, right?*—and gave me a confident wave. Then she threw herself back into dancing. Maybe we'll be friends this year, I thought. But this year doesn't start tonight.

Ed and I were standing alone now, on the outskirts of everyone, excluded from the Herds. I looked at him—his plain, serious face, his skinny body, his carefully styled hair. Was that what I looked like—nerdy, uncomfortable, forgettable as a silly joke?

"You want to dance?" Ed asked. He was staring down at his feet.

"I can't dance."

That's when Charlie slouched past without even seeing me. He had his arm around some girl I didn't know, some beautiful girl who looked old enough for college. I slammed my beer down on the table. Enough. Or pretty soon it would be too much. "Go ahead and dance if you want, Ed. I'm leaving."

I hurried back to the car, which, thanks to Ed's open window, no longer smelled like Mom. Storm clouds rolled above me, scudding across the crescent moon and covering the stars. Watching them, I heard different music in my head—some kind of clashing symphony. And I wanted to drive, drive, drive, farther away than I'd ever been, farther than even Ruth wanted to go.

I started to put down the Firebird's convertible top. But the top got stuck. I was still struggling with it when Ed bumped up against me. I jumped and he jumped, too—away.

"Hey." Ed's face was paler than before; he looked tired. "I guess you've had enough, huh?"

"Let's put it this way." I wiped sweat from my forehead. "I'd rather be anywhere but here."

"Anywhere," Ed agreed.

I gave the top a final tug and it collapsed into place. Then Ed and I got into the car and headed off, chasing clouds that led us only to Cottonwood Lane. We turned down it just as the rain started to fall, heavy drops that seemed to explode on the windshield, on my skin. I pulled over and put the top back up, locked it into place. By this time, I was soaking wet. Ed was watching me from inside the car; he didn't seem inclined to come out into the rain. What have I got to lose? I thought. And I yelled to Ed to wait there, I'd be right back. Lightning flashed; I saw him nod. Relief spread through my chest like a flower opening. There was only one place I really wanted to be, and I was almost there.

I sprinted across the field, past the cottonwoods, then up the hill and down toward the dark smudge that was the little house. I paused at the doorway, which seemed to waver under the force of the gusting wind. Then I went inside.

The rain drummed on the tin roof. Slowly, murkily, things came into focus. There was the sewing machine, a bulky shadow against the wall. Raindrops pinged against its narrow metal back. There was the battered rocker, also spattered with water. These things seemed even lonelier in the darkness, like they more deeply missed the person who had once known them.

Ella. Mom.

I walked slowly to the kitchen, testing floorboards with each step, then through the kitchen to the bedroom. I kept stepping in puddles; each felt like a cold, wet hand grabbing my foot.

Finally I stood beside the iron bed frame. On the wall

in front of me was the painting of the waterfall. Squinting, I managed to make out dark strokes—the letters of her name. Ella would have loved this night, I thought. This night was the kind of night she dreamed of in her dry, thirsty valley. Given a night like this she might have painted other pictures. She wasn't just a woman who wanted the weather to change after all. She must have been much more than that.

But what did I really know?

The shack trembled in the wind, and a gust of rain whisked in through a broken window. I shuddered. I was cold, I realized, in my damp, clinging clothes. I wanted to go back to the car. There was nothing here for me now that Mom was gone. No more secrets to learn from the paintings. No more secrets to share.

I turned from the paintings and screamed. Ed was standing there, his yellow shirt and bandaged hands shimmering, ghostlike, in the beam of the flashlight he balanced in the crook of his elbow.

"You scared the life out of me," I gasped.

"You're still standing." Ed took a step toward me and slipped in a puddle. "Whoa." He turned in slow circles, studying the room. "This place is a trip."

"Who invited you?" My voice sounded harsh.

"I didn't know an invitation was necessary." Ed

focused the light on the paintings, studying each one closely. "Someone sure left their mark."

"Mom," I whispered.

Ed held out his arm to me. In the glare of the flash-light, just past the top of his bandage, I glimpsed the pink rim of a scar.

"You want to dance?" he said, as I carefully took hold of his bandaged hand.

AUGUST 27

On a long drive down a dusty road deep into the country, we pass fields lush with wildflowers and berries. There's the small cup of shelter scooped out of flat, windswept land. And there's the little, abandoned farmhouse that's come to feel like our second home. And here we are inside, seeing the paintings for the first time all over again.

I found Ruth planting chrysanthemums in the park. She didn't seem surprised to see me. She shaded her eyes against the late afternoon sun. "What's up?"she said, like neither of us had ever done anything delinquent, like no one had died.

I said, "I looked for you at Chloe's last night."

Ruth laughed and plunged her spade into the dirt. "Been there, done that."

"So what were you doing instead?"

"I was on the phone."

"Wow."

Ruth ran her fingers through a chrysanthemum's stems, fluffed out the golden buds like hair. "And I was packing. I'm leaving. Tomorrow."

My knees buckled, and I knelt down on the ground beside her. I was getting better at playing it cool. "Where are you off to? Africa? Tibet?"

"Chicago."

"What?"

"Mom and Dad and I have been talking things over. I told them I was either going to run away or I was going to go crazy. That kind of got their attention. So we decided to make some other plans. I've got this aunt who lives in Chicago. She said I could stay with her this fall, go to school there. Mom and Dad said okay. The lesser of several evils, I guess."

"No." I bit my lip, bit back other words. "No way." I had helped a boy out of a car. We were supposed to laugh about things like that.

"Yes way." Ruth sat back on her heels and really looked at me. "You can come and visit if you want."

"I'll think about it."

"Livy, I could go crazy. Or I could run away. Or

maybe I could make myself stay here for a little longer, and then I'd wind up hating this place and hating my parents and maybe even hating you. It might be okay hating Troy City, but I don't particularly want to hate my parents, and I definitely don't want to hate you."

I covered my face with my hands. When I could look up again, I said, "I don't think they have A&Ws in Chicago."

"Damn." Ruth put her arms around me. "I might have to come back for a visit."

AUGUST 28

Mom and I are having a knock-down-drag-out fight. It feels so good. Until I wake up.

*T*his morning: the sound of the wheelbarrow trundling on its flat tire across the grass. I got out of bed and went to the window. And there was Dad, down on his knees and up to his wrists in pine bark chips. He'd planted a slip of a willow tree right where the old one stood. Now he was mulching the roots.

I dressed and went out to him. I watched him work for a while. Finally I said, "You're sure you want another weed?"

Dad looked up at me. He didn't yell at me for being smart. "Yes," was all he said. And then he went back to mulching.

I wanted to thank Dad for planting a willow. I wanted to tell him that I loved willows, too. But before I could, he said, "So what are you going to do today?"

I shrugged. That's not the kind of question Dad usually asked. I didn't know what to say.

He stood up and brushed his hands together. "Don't you think you should do something special, now that you're seventeen?"

I blinked. It's today. My birthday. I'd forgotten.

"It's no big deal," I told him.

But in honor of the day, I planted the redbud in a place I couldn't have imagined visiting, so many weeks ago now, on the day when I first asked Dad if Mom would die—the day I began writing in this journal. I planted the redbud at Mom's grave.

There was no other marker at the site—not yet, anyway. No marble cross or engraved words on a headstone to sum up who Mom was, what she accomplished, her life. There was a fresh, soft patch of green sod. I dug a small hole there and settled the redbud into place. I sat there and tried to imagine springs passing, the pink buds she loved blooming, and me visiting, unafraid.

When I got home, Dad asked me what kind of cake and ice cream I liked, in an obviously casual way. He mentioned that we'd run out of milk again, and bread too, and cereal. He had to go out but he'd be back soon. Don't go anywhere. "What's your favorite color?" he asked. And: "Are you a medium or a large?"

I couldn't imagine what kind of birthday present he was going to find at the grocery store. A pair of socks? A T-shirt? I still can't imagine it, but whatever it is, I'm going to know soon. He's upstairs wrapping it right now—his first time wrapping a gift for me, I bet. He's already spilled out a kitchen drawer searching for tape. I'm thinking: wrinkled paper, snarled ribbon, no card at all. But I guess I should have a little faith in him. Earlier, when he held up my birthday cake and the candles illuminated his face, he reminded me of a broken angel. His broad shoulders cast shadows like battered wings.

I'm sitting on the living room couch, my back to the hospital bed. Soon, Dad says, that bed will be gone. But I can't help but worry that it will become a fixture in this house. Mom was the one who knew how to make things right. Clean things out. Fix things up. Get things ready for tomorrow.

Tomorrow, school starts and I am seventeen. Mom was the one who knew—

There's a gift on the fireplace mantel that I suppose I'm not supposed to notice yet. But of course I saw the envelope tucked beneath the red ribbon, and the writing on it—the script that's so familiar to me. Mom's writing. *Daughter*, she wrote with a shaky flourish. I don't want to guess what's beneath the wrapping, but I can't help but see that it's shaped like this journal.

Write down your dreams, she said. *Write down your dreams and let them tell you what they mean.*

ACKNOWLEDGMENTS:

I am forever grateful to Sara Crowe, agent extraordinaire. Sara, thank you for believing in this novel from the get-go, and especially for keeping the faith. You surely helped me keep mine!

I am also indebted to Jennifer Besser, advocate of my dreams. Your editorial intelligence, kindness, and tact made this journey a true joy, xJ.

Thanks also to Christine Kettner and the other talented folks at Hyperion who wrestle manuscripts into books on a daily basis. I'm so glad that one of them was mine.

Kathi Baron, Julia Buckley, Karen Osborne, Kae Penner-Howell, Lenora Rand, and Martha Whitehead—I deeply appreciate your wise and heartfelt reading. And, Lenora, your lovely home was a godsend when I needed it most.

Gina Frangello, Cecelia Downs, Laura Ruby, and Zoe Zolbrod—your keen insights inspired me through the last revision. Mucho kudos.

Amy Baker, Jan DeVries, Cheryl Hollatz-Wisely, Joni Klein, and Randi Woodworth—ongoing thanks for seeing me through so much in life, and especially for walking this road with me.

Clayton and Joan Halvorsen, you have always embraced my writing, and in doing so, you have always embraced me. I am blessed to have dear parents (and grandparents) like you. And of course, Buddy, too!

Finally, forever and always, Greg, Magdalena, and Teo. God smiled on me and gave me you. Thank you, and love.